DUKE
&
THE LONELY BOY

LYNN LANGAN

Black Rose Writing | Texas

ISBN: 978-1-68433-751-4
PUBLISHED BY BLACK ROSE WRITING
www.blackrosewriting.com

Printed in the United States of America
Suggested Retail Price (SRP) $17.95

Duke & The Lonely Boy is printed in Sabon

*As a planet-friendly publisher, Black Rose Writing does its best to eliminate
unnecessary waste to reduce paper usage and energy costs, while never
compromising the reading experience. As a result, the final word count vs. page count
may not meet common expectations.

For my mom and dad.

DUKE
&
THE LONELY BOY

TOMMY: AGE 17

Funny the thoughts you have when you lie dying. The mind races like a computer program running algorithms of your life's code... Happy, sad, anger, fear, love, resentment...

And then there's that damn Bette Midler song, "The Rose", playing over and over again in my head. Nana would love that if she knew because it is her favorite song in the whole world. "Kind of depressing," I used to say. "A cautionary tale," she would respond.

"Don't forget to be the rose, Tommy," Nan would say, grabbing my cheeks.

But I'm thinking that maybe that Bette lady was right about one thing; that love is a razor that leaves your soul to bleed.

DUKE

Not too many people notice Tommy. He just isn't the noticing type. The way he slinks around school as if he were a shadow instead of a person makes him very easy to miss. And he is the lucky one because it works. I wouldn't have noticed him either if it weren't for the fact that my pre-calc teacher, who happens to be the football coach, insisted that Tommy tutor me. Coach Todd has a way of getting people to do things for him even if that person is a shadow.

Coach Todd has to point out who Tommy even is to me in the crowded cafeteria. He sits alone at one end of a table; the other half is full of other misfortunate kids who are always the butt end of cruel jokes. He doesn't look like them. He isn't covered in acne, or dressed in all black, or in clothes from the last decade, or any other stereotype boxes we put those kids in. He is just alone. And if he were to stand up and sit in any other seat, he would blend in.

He intimidates me. Not physically, I have height and weight against his skinny frame and could easily take him in a fight. But his quiet existence reminds me of someone who is bored because high school isn't enough, and our childish ways are beneath him. I think about asking Coach Todd for a new tutor but dread the speech he'll give followed up with extra reps on the field.

Coach Todd arranges for us to meet in the school library by the computers. By the time I get there I've convinced myself that this was about the worst idea anyone had ever had. This shadow is going to judge me as some dumb jock who can't figure out math and, by the way, it is my mom's fault too for making me take the stupid class so I can get into college. I hate all three of them: Tommy, Coach Todd, and my mom.

I'm in a really bad mood. I should be on the field practicing instead of taking a seat across from him at the table. But then Tommy does something unexpected. He tells me a joke. It goes like this:

Beaker from the Muppets went to a disco last night. They played "The Twist", he did that, they played "Jump", he did that, they played "Come on, Eileen", he got kicked out for that.

The librarian kicks us out because I can't stop laughing and I'm causing a ruckus in her library. Turns out there is a person casting that shadow all along and, man, is he funny in an unexpected way. Maybe this whole getting-help-in-math thing won't be so bad after all.

"Where to now?" I ask as I follow him down the hallway.

"Cafeteria."

"Thanks for doing this," I say to him as we walk.

"No problem. It will look good on the college applications." His voice is back to flat like he didn't just tell that joke.

We walk quietly the remainder of the way and grab the first table we see. There are other students using the space as well. Tucked up in the far-right corner is the cheer squad. A pang of anxiety fills my stomach. For one thing, I should be on the football field practicing, and for the other thing, Kristy locks eyes with mine.

Kristy. The head cheerleader and the most complicated girl on Earth. And now she sees me with Tommy probably wondering what the hell I'm doing here. We've only been together for over a month, but it feels a whole lot longer than that. I wish I could jog up to her and tell her why Tommy and I are here, but I know I can't. And I would have told her about the tutoring thing if we could talk like a normal couple, but we also can't do that. And it's not like Kristy's telling me what I can or cannot do; it's her father who pulls the strings. And it's not because I'm black and her father wouldn't like that; it's the fact that I don't belong to her church and her father doesn't approve of any boy outside of their religion.

"Do you want to go back to the library?" Tommy asks. "Because I need you to concentrate."

3

"I'm fine."

"Okay. But just so you know you've been staring at Kristy for a while now." He rearranges his textbook on the table.

"It's not what you think." I grab my school bag, debating whether or not I would prefer the library.

"So, it's not like you guys have been secretly seeing each other or anything?" He looks over at Kristy, and I immediately want to run out of the cafeteria.

I want to follow his stare, but I'm so nervous she is looking back at him. Every inch of my body fires up and I can feel the sweat starting to form on the back of my neck.

"It's not like that. We're just friends." I sneak a look over to Kristy, who has a death grip on her pompoms. I know people talk about us and normally I don't care, but for the first time since this whole thing between us started, I feel a little anger toward her. It is one thing to not tell parents about the dating but trying to pretend we are not a thing around our friends is stupid. "Why do you think we're together?"

"Just a guess." He pulls his calculator from his bag.

"Why would you guess that?"

"I'm messing with you. When you two first got together it was all the talk, but now I guess everyone has grown bored with it."

"We're not together."

"Okay. That's not what everyone says. They say her dad wouldn't approve of you."

"It's not a black and white thing if that's what you're thinking. And we're just friends."

"That's not what I was thinking, that's what everyone is saying." Tommy's glare cuts through me.

"Gossip is just that: gossip."

"You realize that lying about this just makes you look stupid. Maybe if you weren't you and she wasn't the captain of the cheer team, you could go unnoticed, but unfortunately you have all eyes on you. Stop lying and just own it."

"Just shut up and teach me some math." Now my blood is boiling. I don't like this side of me, the side that told this kid to shut up. This side of me is hateful and hurtful and it's new to me. And I feel like I don't have control over it.

"I didn't mean to get you mad. I was only saying you shouldn't have to lie about it, that's all. If that's how her dad feels that would be messed up. But since you're just friends, then no big deal. And anyway, who am I to say a word?"

"Yeah, who the hell are you?"

"No one. Sorry for talking. Now if you could open your book to chapter three, that would be a huge help," he says.

"Her dad is a religious nut, okay? I'm not from her church so you see the problem, right?" I'm getting the nervous leg twitch I get whenever I know my back is against the wall. "Why the hell am I explaining this to you? How do you even know any of this? You act like you don't care about school."

It's strange how comfortable I feel finally confessing to someone that I am really seeing her instead of the absurd lies I have to tell. I'm so sick of lying. And who is this kid going to tell? He basically doesn't exist in this school. No one would believe him if he did say something.

"Be careful with her. Maybe she's lying to you, trying to create some drama. She seems like the drama type. Remember when she had that kid suspended for supposedly leaving those notes in her locker? That poor kid didn't leave any inappropriate notes, but she made such a big deal out of it that the school had to do something."

"What the hell do you even know about her?" My fists are balled up, ready to strike. This tutoring business isn't going to work. I'll have to find a new tutor after I kill him. I catch Kristy out of the corner of my eye. She's looking this way. Immediately I stand and tell the skinny asshole we're going back to the library where we will promise to be quiet.

"I have a quiz tomorrow, so I need you today, but then I'll find someone else to help me," I say right before walking in the quiet space. We find seats at an already occupied table.

"Duke, I'm sorry," Tommy whispers. "I just think it's messed up. I mean, even if her parents are religious nuts, she could still be in a relationship with you. That's all I'm saying. Everyone around school talks about it so I guess I just thought I could too. My bad. No more personal stuff. Just math."

And he keeps to his word. Later that night when I'm brushing my teeth it occurs to me that Tommy is the only person I know from school that has pointed out how messed up it was with Kristy. Yet he said the whole school talks about it. That must mean my friends talk about it and no one said shit to my face. That's kind of screwed up.

I guess that's not true. My sister has said plenty about how she doesn't like her, but that's just white noise. Jayla breaks my balls whenever she gets a chance. I just wish everyone could see how great Kristy is when we aren't hiding our relationship. No one sees the notes she slips in my locker telling me to have a good practice or have an amazing game. She gets me.

All they think they see is us trying to cover up our feelings for each other. And now even Tommy thinks he can weigh in on this. I wish everyone could just let us be. But I need Tommy, I know that. And Coach won't understand why I want a new tutor. Everything in life seems like I just have to suck it up and deal with it. Too bad about your feelings, Duke.

The next day I get my first C in pre-calc instead of the usual F. At lunch, I spot Tommy and tell him I'll see him again in the library. His face lights up with a crooked, small smile. He might be an odd person, but he sure can teach.

TOMMY: AGE 17

When I wake up, I think I'm in the hospital, but I can't keep my eyes open long enough to confirm. Instead, I go down the rabbit hole chasing after memories that somehow came undone. They are like thousand-legged bugs crawling into my brain, tickling the receptors to wake, trying to recover the past; like an archaeologist unearthing a precious artifact delicately trying not to chip a clue that connects us all. "Everything connects," Pop would say. Every time I get a lead, get close to whatever the hell the brain is trying to tell me, however the pieces are to fit together, some new thought shifts, and the current thought is scrubbed clean of details then perhaps dipped into lead because they always seem heavy as they float away. And even when I fight to hold on to them, because they belong to me, I often have to drop them because I feel my bones splintering under the sheer weight and know to just them let go.

I know I want to be at my grandparent's house. I need the comfort of their home. The old Victorian with long hallways and little rooms packed full of all their family history. Pop's garage tucked out back past the sprawling green yard. Not too long ago we had been working on an old Ford pickup from the early eighties that he found for a bargain. "Young buck didn't know what he was selling," Pop would say to anyone that would listen. He would tell them how he drove into God's country to an estate sale and they just wanted to off load it. Nan wasn't happy about how much the tow truck company robbed them to have it hauled back to their place. She had a way of appearing at the right spot in his story to add this little detail in. She reminded me of the person who plays the triangle in a band. The whole time you never noticed the person standing there holding that little piece of metal and then just at the perfect pause they ding it and bring you right into their focus.

That truck become what I did on Saturdays for a year straight. The winters were terrible because the cold stung my throat and the summers were unbearable with heat by the afternoon. But the perfect spring morning with fresh-cut grass or the chilly fall morning with all the golden colors of the leaves turning made it all worth it. That and the truck. The smell of the oil and my grandfather's cigar burning endlessly in an ashtray that was as old as he was. "Tommy," he would say tugging at his white beard, "we are going to make this puppy run again."

My hands were calloused from all the wrenching, a term my Pop loved throwing out. Those Saturdays were spent in his modest garage jam-packed with tools, dollies, lift kits, and spare parts. The old work bench full of knot holes, cluttered with notes, small tools, stains, and half started projects that always drew me in with wonder. This garage was the safest place I've ever known. It reminded me of a mother's womb: small and warm with just the right amount of space. In the winter, we were protected from the cold by a kerosene heater that somehow overtook the natural aroma of greasy parts. Hours spent watching his leather hands clench wrenches and turn with all his might while cursing under his breath. When he was too frustrated, he'd hand me the tool and tell me to use my young muscles, but careful not to strip the bolt.

That's what it's like unearthing these memories. But I stay focused on the smell of the garage and his voice and what it all means because it must mean something. He worries about me. I could see that in the way he studies my face when he thinks I'm preoccupied. He tightens his jaw as if he is biting down on something, maybe it is just his guilt for feeling like he failed somewhere as a parent.

And in so many ways he did. My mother.

I want to stay here longer, but I feel the drugs wearing off. I know my eyes will focus soon enough. The weight of the world crashing down around me. The pain starts in my legs and slithers its way up; knees on fire, thighs tight with knots, penis uncomfortably aware it's not alone, stomach full of bricks, arms that tingle, neck stiff, brain on fire.

Eyelids fight to stay closed.

Wide awake.

The white walls bathe me. The constant beeping from the machines reminds me of time. Tubes sticking out of me. Is that my blood?

Someone is saying my name and telling me to stay with them. I want to speak but can't.

I have questions, but the words seem to be melting in my brain. They float over clouds and drift off to sea. I have questions.

The fuchsia swirls of wispy clouds drawn down by the force of midnight-blue storm fingers grabbing every piece of me that might remember until my mother is standing before me. "Tommy," she says, "come with me. I want to show you something."

DUKE

It has been a week since Tommy has been tutoring me and so far, I produced another very high C on a quiz. The librarian has left us alone for the most part. She still likes to circle our table as a preemptive warning she will kick us out if there is any laughter.

"This shit is so hard. Why can't I just get it?" I whisper.

"It's a funny thing to realize that teachers sometimes can't teach. Or at least teach to everyone in their classroom," Tommy whispers back. "It seems to me like you're just missing some of the steps. We just have to find which steps they are and then this will all come together for you."

He dissects each problem like a surgeon looking for a bleeder until he finds the step I don't understand, and then he fully explains it to me in words that make sense. Sometimes when he is in his own head trying to find the right words to give me, I can see this little patch of sadness streak across his face. A fleeting moment. At first, I thought it was him trying so hard to dumb down the material that he actually felt bad for me, but then I noticed it would happen when he talked to the librarian. He is a meteor shower of sorrow.

I've seen this look before. My cousin, Larry, who moved in with us not long ago, watched his best friend get shot dead in front of him. The elders in the family decided Larry should be surrounded by family at all times since his parents moved away a few years back. My parents volunteered their house because Jayla and I were closer to his age and less likely to say the wrong things like our younger cousins. The first few weeks after he moved in, he would get spooked if a car door shut outside. Mom had to constantly tell me and my sister to gently shut doors in the house and not to slam cabinets shut. He wasn't all there mentally. You could tell he was having a thousand conversations in his head at once. On more than one occasion he tried to stay awake for twenty-four hours because his dreams tormented him, but the lack of sleep made him speak in tongues. Dad finally brought home a case of beer, which he drank until he passed out, his long, lanky body sprawled in the lawn chair.

My dad said avoidance can make the mind numb enough to start packing away evil things and help reshape the events of tragedy. But there are still moments when it flashes against his face and I know he is slow-dancing with the gun.

My cousin told me once, breath soaked full of beer, that when his friend died, he shit and pissed himself. He said, "We are all babies, don't you see? These limbs of ours grow and we march towards death every day, but at the very essence of us we are infants in this grand galaxy. We come in and go out the same way—shitting and pissing. We always need. Always. We are always afraid. Always."

I'm not convinced of his theory, but then again, he saw death firsthand, so what do I really know? Maybe I haven't experienced anything. That would be Larry's argument to me. But as he said, the needing and the fear haven't shown up at my door yet. We looked up into the dark sky; he seemed to search for more clues to the universe, and for the first time in my life I felt small and somewhat incomplete.

It bothers me that Tommy doesn't care about filling in the normal spaces of silences. I know I told him to only talk about math, but it's weird that he never tries to make an effort. Once the clock hits three pm, he's packing his bag. There is something in him that doesn't want to connect. The part that bothers me in these moments of silence is the overwhelming feeling of desperation, and I'm never sure if it is mine or his.

And if I'm honest, it's really aggravating.

"Same time tomorrow?" Tommy asks.

"Oh no, I forgot to tell you I can't come after school. Can you meet up on Saturday afternoon?"

"Sure. Give me your number just in case."

I tell my number as he programs it into his phone. He texts me an empty bubble so I have his number. He tells me he'll see me there and walks away. Such a strange dude. When I leave the library, Kristy is waiting right outside the doors.

"Why are you going to practice late?" she demands. "What are you doing here?"

"Why do you care?" Her impatient attitude rubs me the wrong way.

"What do you mean, why do I care? I care because you're missing practice."

"If I could talk to you outside of these walls, then maybe you would know."

"Why are you being a jerk, Duke?"

"You know everyone talks about us as if we are some kind of joke. And I never get to see you anymore."

"Holy shit, what is with you? You know I had the church function last weekend and since when did you start caring about what everyone says? I thought that shit didn't matter to you."

"I don't care what people say, but I would like to spend time with my girlfriend, if that's what you are." My voice is sharp and full of anger.

"I don't know what is with you! I was just concerned about you, that's all. But clearly you need to get over yourself." She turns and walks away.

"Kristy, wait." I jog up to her. "Do you really care?"

She studies my face for a moment and then kisses me. Her soft lips steady me. "Of course, I care."

"I have a tutor, that's all, to help make sure I get into college." I pull her all the way into me, resting my chin on her shoulder. Every time I'm this close to her I feel calm and strong.

"I got to get back to cheer." She kisses me and leaves. The silent hallway gives me peace. Everything is okay. I need to stop overreacting to things.

On the field, I am bulletproof. No worries of math or Kristy entering my mind. The minute my cleats dig into the turf, I leave all the weight of life behind me. I'm an astronaut, weightless, and far out of reach of everyday problems. Zeroed in on the ball and whoever is in my way of the end zone. My parents always ask me if I can hear them cheering from the stands. No. I hear my heartbeat, the play calls, and nothing else.

The late September air has a cool chill to it already. We win the game and remain undefeated. Kristy blows a kiss in my general direction; of course, this was all she could do since her dad and stepmom are in the stands. And really at this moment I don't care because I had three touchdown receptions, and nothing is more important than that.

My dad catches up to me before I can get into the school. Between breaths, he tells me how interested the scouts are after tonight's game.

"Stop running," he says.

"Why? I have to get into the locker room before Coach Todd freaks out."

"Coach Todd is talking to them. Look at me, Duke." He grabs my pads. "I'm so proud of you. Next year you'll be playing at some university. Let's just take it in right now." He throws his arms around me for a big hug.

"Thanks, Dad. And we did it. Me and you."

"Now you just trying to get tears. Not going to happen." He slaps the back of my helmet. "See you at home."

After Coach Todd talks to us, we are released back to the real world. Everyone is heading back to Tim's house to celebrate, but I find Kristy sitting in her car parked outside the gymnasium doors.

"Hop in," she says.

"Where we going?" I ask.

"It's a surprise." She floors the gas of her stepmom's minivan. We fly down the back entrance of school, smashing over the speed bumps, all the while her twin sister's toys bounce and rattle around.

"Maybe you should slow down." I fumble around, trying to latch my seat belt.

"No time." She drives faster.

She hurries off campus and down the quiet street until we come to a business complex, which she abruptly turns into and parks in the first spot. We sit there under the light, tight in the parking spot as if there are going to be more cars pulling in any minute.

"So, what's this about?" I ask, looking at her. Taking her all in. Her soft, brown hair tucked tight in a ponytail all done up in her cheer uniform.

"I just wanted to kiss you."

"Oh really?" My stomach buzzes with excitement.

"Yeah, but first I've been thinking about what you said the other day. It does make me sad that we don't get to hang out and go on dates like a normal couple. And I haven't really thought about how that makes you feel." She sits all the way back in the driver's seat.

"I mean, it doesn't feel great sometimes." I sigh. "It's difficult. I want to be able to do things with you and not always be so secretive."

"Do you still want to be with me even though I can't give you what you want?"

"And what is it that you think I want?"

"For me to be your girlfriend for the whole world to see?"

"You're not some kind of prize, Kristy. I don't want to drape you over my arm and walk you around. I just want to be able to have a normal relationship."

"You didn't answer the question."

"Yes, I still want to be with you. Do you still want to be with me?"

"Duke, come on, of course I want to be with you. I brought you, here didn't I?"

"You brought me to an empty parking lot. You could be planning on killing me for all I know." I laugh.

"You know me so well." She smiles. "I brought you here to kiss you."

"Then what's with all the words?" I lean over and pull her into me. "I'm in this, even if it is complicated. I was just in a bad mood the other day."

"I forgive you then." She gently touches my face. "Don't let it happen again."

"Shut up already."

"Is that how you talk to your girlfriend?"

"It is now."

"You really are the best boyfriend." And with that she kisses me, and the world falls away.

THE ORIGINAL WRECK: PART ONE

TOMMY: AGE 8

If all problems could be boiled down to one moment and a solution tucked into a nanosecond and if only we could have the ability to see this glimmer of time, maybe then we could change the world—more importantly our own tiny world we exist in. I was dirty. Hungry. Tired. It was so late at night and I remembered being ripped from my bed. Filthy sheets. Sleep stuck on my eyes. Her tugging my arm. "Move faster," she yelled. It was the first time all day she was awake. I spent the entire day watching television, periodically checking on her as she laid in a dream state on the couch. She had been spending a lot of days like this lately. When she was awake, she either hated me very much or loved me unconditionally. But on this night, I knew it was not the latter.

I hoped it was just a run to the convenience store for her menthol cigarettes but when we drove right on by my stomach began to hurt—partially out of hunger and the fleeting hope of buying something to eat and partially out of dread of what seedy place she was driving us to. She rocked in her seat as if she were in a rocking chair, and it unnerved me to see my mother cradle herself. Her fingers wrapped tightly around the steering wheel while she spoke in tongue like she was saying prayers to God himself. A plea, I thought.

The houses on the street were crammed tight like if you wanted to borrow sugar all you had to do was open a window and tap on your neighbor's. Mom was irritated that parking couldn't just be easy; but I suspected nothing was easy for her at that moment with all those jumpy nerves coursing through her body. I knew it wasn't right. Other adults never jittered when I was around them.

She scraped the curb with the tires in her haste when she finally found a suitable parking space. She whacked the door open with her shoulder, which normally she would have something to say along the lines of "this piece of shit Toyota falling apart," but she had no time for extra words—she must have thought they'd slow her down. Slamming the door shut, she raced across the street and onto a porch that housed two ratty sofas occupied by three men. I unbuckled my seatbelt and crawled up to the driver's seat because the back doors didn't open after they were hit on two different occasions. I watched as she straddled one of the men. From my view behind the smoke-coated window, I could see her shirt being ripped off her. She wiggled to try and free herself, back and forth she flung her body.

I slammed the door open, knowing what I had to do. "Mom," I screamed.

The man stood with her still attached to his body. He slammed her up against the house and she let out a moan of pain. I ran faster across the street. One of the other men opened the screen door, allowing for Mom to be carried into the house. I took the steps to the front porch two at a time, all the while screaming after her, my tears stinging my face.

"Hey, little man." The man who opened the door grabbed my shirt. "What's the rush?" He forcefully guided me to one of the couches the other man was sitting on.

"I need to get my mom; that man was hurting her." I tried freeing myself from his grip.

"He wasn't hurting her. She was having fun. Adult fun. Just sit here with us and hang out, little bro." He sat next to me, wedging me between the two of them. "What's your name?"

"Tommy," I answered.

I was trapped, and they knew it. We were sitting so close I could feel their leg muscles relax when they realized I was no longer a threat to them. They cracked open cans of beer and offered me some. I knew I wasn't allowed because Grandpa always told me no when I asked for his, but this night seemed to give me permission and I was thirsty after screaming so I took a tiny sip.

We sat on the couch long enough for them to drink all the beer and crack open more when the monster came out of the house. "Chris," was all he said, but he pointed toward the door as if saying *go*.

His voice made my skin crawl. He made his way to Chris's seat and sat next to me, sweaty with no shirt on. The hatred this man instilled in me was almost unbearable except the beer he forced me to drink made my brain tingle with an ease of carelessness.

I woke up on the couch with the morning sun glaring in my face. My shirt was missing and so were my shoes. Mom laid very still on the other couch. I strained my eyes to see if she was breathing. The rise and fall of her chest was barely there, if there at all. Fear paralyzed me from doing the rational thing, which would have been to jump up immediately and check; instead, I cried, hoping she would hear me. When she still didn't move, I convinced myself she was dead, but I needed to check.

She laid in just her underwear and bra, vomit caked all over her body and face. "Mom." I shook her. A little cry escaped her mouth. Relief filled my soul, making me want to help, but I didn't know how and no one else was on the porch with us.

The front door was open, allowing for bugs and intruders to walk right in. I pushed the door all the way open and stepped into the living room. On the couch, Chris snored, with one of his hands stuffed down his underpants. I kept moving through the rest of the small house, looking for someone who was awake. Room after room, beer cans and cigarette butts laid all over the nasty carpet. There were also needles strewn about haphazardly, waiting to be accidentally stepped on. No one else was there, so I had to go back and wake Chris up.

"I think my mom is sick," I said, hovering above him. I didn't want to touch him in fear he might retaliate. He didn't budge, forcing me to repeat myself several times and louder each time I did until he woke up.

"What?" he asked. "Where is she?" He slowly moved his feet off the couch until he was sitting. "Outside," I said. "She's covered in puke."

"That's bad." He jumped up and grabbed his pants off the recliner, jamming his feet into them and throwing on his shirt. "Where are my shoes?" He had dark circles under his pale blue eyes. "Little bro, find my shoes." He jogged to the front porch as I searched under the piss-soaked couch and pulled a pair of sneakers out.

When I found him on the porch, his face was pale. "She barely has a heartbeat. I'm sorry, bro, but I'm out of here. You need to get help. You got to find her cell phone and call 911. Good luck." He ripped the shoes out of my hands and ran off the porch and down the street.

I sat next to her for a minute, trying to think of where her purse was when I caught our car out of the corner of my eye. I ran down the steps and ripped open the front door, finding her purse on the passenger seat. I dumped all the contents out to expose the phone.

"911, what is your emergency?" a woman's voice filled the receiver.

"Something is wrong with my mom," I answered.

"What's your location?"

"I don't know," I said, looking around for a street sign.

"It's okay, sweetie, the police are coming now. What is wrong with your mom?"

"She can't really move and she's covered in throw up." I could hear the sirens coming. "I got to go." I hung the phone up and ran back to the house to search for my shirt and shoes, which I found in the bathroom. After putting them on, I raced out to the porch and was greeted by the cops, who were crowded over my mother. They didn't notice me until she was strapped onto the gurney. Only then did they realize they had more of a problem than they thought.

DUKE

Saturdays are always workout days. Sure, we needed to rest after a game, but resting would have to wait until offseason. We were in the playoff hunt and nothing could stand in the way of getting extra reps in. Tim picked me up at exactly ten a.m. because in Tim's world, timing is everything. How many steps does it take me to get open? How many seconds does he have until the opposing team breaks the line and sacks him? Timing. He's my best friend, who happens to be the quarterback. We are the dynamic duo and have been since Pop Warner. He throws, I catch.

I can hear the bass to his stereo thumping as I shut the front door. I already know it's going to be a tough workout. When he gets this way, he doesn't take shortcuts, doesn't let a rep slide, or skip that last bit of cardio. On days like this my blood runs hot with ash and ember. I am not human; I am a machine being fueled by competition being shoveled in like coal on an old locomotive. Shovel, burn, repeat.

I take my seat, always in the passenger seat, never in the back. This is an agreement between us that we never talked about; a level of respect that comes with being friends with someone as long as we have. He's kicked many people to the back seat whenever they tried to call shotgun.

We pick up Smookler, the center for the team, and drive to the gym. At this hour, we basically have the place to ourselves. Just us and some old folks who would never use the equipment we're on. We talk only on little breaks and mostly about our next game and how to win. Two hours later, we carb out on pancakes at Johnny's Diner, our favorite.

"What's up with you and Kristy?" Smookler asks, shoveling half a pancake in his mouth, the syrup dripping down his chin and onto the table. "I saw you leave with her last night."

"Nothing's up. She was just giving me a ride home," I answer.

"Oh, here we go with the 'nothing is going on between us' bullshit. Everyone knows, Duke. She's not that quiet about it," Tim says. "Girls talk."

"Let them talk," I say, pushing my food around on the plate.

"I don't get it. Just admit it to us already. It's kind of embarrassing that you don't," Smookler adds.

"Or insulting." Tim looks directly at me. "We are your best friends and you won't even tell us."

"Do you want me to get you a BFF necklace?" I answer defensively. But I can see it in his eyes, the fact is he's bothered by this.

How could I not tell my best friend? I know this lie is dividing us a little. But isn't that all it takes? One fault line and the whole land sits and waits for the moment the one rock shifts in the wrong direction—then boom—earthquake. I don't want that with Tim.

"Fine. We are together." I breathe a sigh of relief.

"Oh, shit! You actually admitted it." Smookler chokes a little on the food in his mouth. "Pay up, bitch." He puts his open palm up on the table. Tim digs in his wallet and pulls out a twenty-dollar bill and slaps it into his hand.

"What the hell?" My cheeks burn.

"Nothing personal, Duke. Money is money." Smookler slips the bill into his sweatpants pocket.

I want to flip the table.

"Yo, I'm sorry, Duke," Smookler says. "It really wasn't about the money. We were just getting concerned that you would keep covering this whole thing up. What's the big deal anyway? Her dad?"

"Yup," I answer, still debating whether to break something. Tim hasn't even looked at me. I feel disgusting. I broke the promise I had with Kristy for what? Twenty bucks.

"Details." Smookler spits tiny pieces of chewed food from his mouth.

"That's all you get," I answer. "You guys are assholes."

"Calm down. We didn't mean to hurt your feelings," Smookler says, pretending to wipe tears from his eyes. "And there's probably no details because you ain't getting shit. Little kisses," Smookler says, puckering his lips.

"More than you." I take a long-exaggerated drink of water, hoping he'll change the subject, which he does because he bores easily.

They may have gotten me to confess, but they will never get details from me. I've had my mom yelling at me for years on this very subject. To disrespect a woman is the worst offense in her book, second to murder. And even when I say I would never do that she still raises her voice as if I already did and yells at me some more. My sister laughs and laughs as if this is the funniest thing to her. Little sisters are annoying, especially when they are only two years younger than you.

Tim picks his phone up off the table and begins going over the college football games that are on today. The two of them talk stats and players as I feel myself sink into the cushion of the bench. The rest of breakfast is a blur.

After we drop Smookler off, Tim lowers the radio.

"I'm sorry about the bet. That wasn't cool," he says.

"No worries."

"Yeah, still, I'm sorry. That was messed up. I really didn't think you'd admit it."

"Can you not say anything?" I've felt sick about the confession ever since. All I need is either of these assholes to repeat what I said and put Kristy in a bad spot at home.

"You already made us swear up and down to the football gods. We aren't going to say a word. But everyone knows, so what's the big deal?"

"I don't want Kristy getting mad. We promised not to tell anyone."

"Whatever you want, Duke. But I think it's sort of crazy. If everyone knows, then it shouldn't be a big deal. She's making this harder than it needs to be."

"It is what it is," I answer.

When I get home, I text Kristy to see if she wants to hang out for a little bit. She replies she's stuck in family zone for the weekend. She always complains about the twins because they are two-year-old who don't have friends or a social life. Whenever there is a Saturday night adult church function, she's stuck babysitting. So, her night consists of animated movies and diaper changes while her parents get to go out.

In the kitchen, I make myself a peanut butter and jelly sandwich while Jayla fills me in on the sophomore gossip. It's so funny how many worlds fit into one school building. She looks shocked that I didn't hear about the cheating scandal in Ms. Dubin's French class. She keeps talking even though I'm falling asleep at the table. I think she's still talking as I walk down the hallway past Larry, who already claimed the couch as a napping place, and dive headfirst into my bed.

I wake up from my nap by my phone buzzing in my pocket. Tommy Moffe's name is blurry to my sleep-filled eyes.

"Yo," I answer.

"Hey, Duke, it's me Tommy." His voice fills my ear.

"I know."

"Are we still on for meeting at the library at three?"

"What?"

"You said on Thursday that you couldn't meet after school but that you wanted to cram for the test coming up. Remember?"

"Barely. But, yeah, I do want to meet up still," I say, my voice not hiding the disappointment. Saturdays are for anything not school related.

I walk the two miles to the library. Both parents are out, leaving no rides and no cars to borrow. I don't think I've walked to this place since I was twelve. And I only did that because Mom insisted that I take Jayla who found a library book under her bed that she borrowed and never returned months ago. Mom decided the only way Jayla was going to learn her lesson was if she walked it off. Too bad for me that Jayla wasn't old enough to go it alone. That's the downside of siblings— sometimes you have to be their keeper.

I find Tommy where he'd said he'd be—all the way in the back by the big windows. The place is busier than I expected but then again, I never come here on a Saturday to know people would actually be here.

He waits with a still face, the math book opened, and a calculator perched on top of an opened notebook. My legs are heavy from the workout and walk, anchoring my feet to the carpet like cinderblocks.

He wants to dive into math, and I want to lie on the ground and take another nap.

"Did you come to the game last night?" I ask, hoping to slow this down.

"No."

"We won. Still undefeated."

"That's good."

"I had three touchdowns and there were scouts there."

He looks over his notes, his ice-blue eyes never indicating that anything in this life is interesting. I could have said I saved a life on the field or took one, and I don't think his reaction would change.

"It's a big deal for me," I say under my breath.

"I know. All the more reason we need to work harder to get you to pass this test." He finally looks up at me and somewhere in those artic eyes, I see a fleck of fire.

"What I said before about not talking because of what you said about Kristy, I don't mean it. I was just mad."

"Sorry," he says, looking away.

"Let's just have a redo. Act like it never happened."

"Okay."

"But don't talk about her again."

"Deal."

He is relentless. My brain is on fire like my other muscles, but he keeps pushing me. We are finally kicked out when the library closes. I watch as he walks toward his truck and then I start the long walk home.

From behind me, I hear the hum of a motor and the slight squeak of breaks. "Get in."

"This is a sweet truck." I place my backpack in the middle of the front bench. "It's a classic."

"My grandfather and I built this engine up."

"Really?" I don't know what to be more impressed with, the fact that Tommy knows how to work on cars, or the fact that he finally told me something personal about himself.

"You're shocked."

"Well, no offense, it seems like you're more into books then building an engine."

"No offense taken. I mostly watched him work, but I did learn a lot."

"That's pretty cool, though. And he gave it to you instead of selling it?"

"Sort of."

I can tell he's done talking about it, so I give him directions to my house to change the conversation. We rattle down the road in silence. When we pull up, he tells me next time he'll just pick me up in the first place.

THE ORIGINAL WRECK: PART ONE CONTINUED

TOMMY: AGE 8

That morning was my ninth birthday, my first hangover, and the day I went to live with my grandparents.

There was a series of events that led up to me being able to stay with my grandparents, but I don't remember much of it. Here's what I remember: the ride home in the back seat of my grandparents' Buick, conversation lacking, the silence seemed to actually be another person in the car, the person we weren't supposed to talk about which was my mother who we left in the hospital. Walking through their front door and smelling the fireplace reek that always seemed more prevalent when it rained and at some point, during the many hours at the hospital, it began raining. Nan asking if we wanted coffee and then saying I couldn't drink any when I was the only one who replied yes, and Pop saying he'd be right back, he was going to collect some of my belongings from my house.

When he returned, he carried plastic shopping bags filled with new clothes; he told Nan there was nothing viable at Sammy's house, my mother, for me to use. I could have told him that before he left if he asked me, but he didn't ask because he couldn't look me in the face, at least not since he and Nan had the private conversation with a lady while I waited in the room with Mom.

Nan made my bed up in Aunt Tammy's old room and not Mom's, which we didn't have a conversation about, even though I first went to Mom's room, out of habit. She tucked me under the warm flannel blankets and kissed me on the forehead.

"Happy birthday," she whispered. "I didn't want you to think we forgot with all the mess going on." She cinched the blankets up closer to my face. "This Friday, we'll have a birthday party and cake."

Pop leaned against the door frame; his face sagged even further down than usual. He sighed and began to speak but stopped and shook his head as if maybe the thoughts were likened to a Magic 8-Ball and he could shake around until the right saying floated to the top.

"I got this present for you." He walked toward my bed, reminding me of a cowboy in those old country westerns. "It's a sketch pad and some colored pencils." He handed me the gift that was still in the plastic store bag. "I know how much you like drawing."

"Thank, Pop, I really love it." I pulled the contents out of the bag and spread them out over the blanket, picking up the colored pencils to busy my hands while Nan left the room.

"Tommy." Pop sighed again. "Do you have any questions about what's happening to your mom?"

"No," I answered, but of course I did. I had a million questions and no voice.

"I see," he mumbled. "Well, in case you were wondering, she'll be going away for a little bit and then coming to live here with us for some time."

"Okay," I replied.

"The thing is, Tommy, what do you know about addiction?" he asked.

"Not much, I guess."

"That's okay. You shouldn't know anything about it, but the thing is you saw some things that you shouldn't have, I think. Your mom is a little sick and we are going to get her better, but I just wanted to let you know that if you want to talk about anything, Nan and I are here for you."

"Okay, Pop." I answered. He leaned over and kissed my forehead before leaving.

My birthday party wasn't really what I had in mind. I was thinking more like roller rink or movies whereas the grandparents planned just cake and ice cream at the house with my cousins: Alex, Shan, and Lily. Alex was two months older than me and Shan one year younger. Their little sister, Lily, was only five, and I found her extremely annoying because she wouldn't stop asking where my mom was.

After the cake ceremony of blowing out the nine blue candles that burned a yellow glow, I slipped outside and wandered to Pop's garage. I didn't dare open the door because at that time I thought a hidden treasure must be tucked in there for all the guarding against any grandchild going in there. Summer was slipping away, the evidence in the low sun tucking itself to sleep at such an early hour of 8:30. I could hear the tail end of my cousin's conversation drifting up from the depths of the basement and wafting out the open windows across the lawn. They were talking about me and how I live here now. But there was another voice tangling in with theirs and it was much closer; like a hunter, I strained my ears for clues. It was a girl's voice, and she seemed upset about something, so I tracked her voice to the edge of the garage where I remained incognito. Ever so carefully, I peered around the corner and saw her there with a shovel in her hand and fresh soil by her feet. She carried a carefully wrapped package as she stared into the earth. Her tears streaked her dirt-covered face as she muttered words to what I could see now to be a red-and-white striped towel.

"Hey," I said. My tiny voice threatened her moment of grief. Not sure if she even heard me, I cleared my voice and tried again. "Hey, you."

"I heard you the first time." Her eyes remained fixed on the soil. "I'm trying to bury my friend in peace."

"I'm sorry." I didn't move back into hiding though; I was too curious to know what she was putting to rest. "I've never been to a funeral."

"Well, they are very sad and very private," she answered. We stood there silent. I knew I should have moved backed but something about this moment made sense to me. Inside, the adults were most likely discussing me, and I knew my cousins were too, so the only place I belonged was right in this sad girl's moment. "Well, if you're going to watch, you should just come over then. You can help me cover the hole before my parents find out anyway."

"Okay." I walked over to her and looked into the hole she dug. "Who died?"

"I found another mouse on one of the glue boards in the basement. He tried chewing his leg off, but I guess he got his face stuck on the pad. Did you ever see a glue board? They are awful. The mouse runs on, gets stuck, every time he tries to move, more of him gets stuck, and then all he has is time. Time to starve to death. I begged my parents not to put these down there and I've been doing my best to find them and throw them away before anyone gets hurt, but last night I slept at Suzy's house and they must have put this trap down."

"That's really terrible. He tried to eat his own leg off. Why would your parents do that? Do they know what happens to the mice when they get stuck?" I moved closer to her.

"My father is an exterminator." She placed the mouse in the hole. "I'm Roxy."

"Tommy," I answered.

"You know what else, Tommy," she kicked some loose soil, "they get mad when I bury them. They think I'm destroying the grass by digging these holes. They want to put the mouse in the trash like that's all his mouse life deserved: rolled-up glue trap shoved in the garbage to forever remain stuck to the trap."

"Isn't he on the trap now?" I asked.

"No!" She looked at me, crossed as if I were on her parents' side.

"I'm sorry. It seemed a little flat like cardboard."

"If you must know, I take scissors and cut around the body. I tried once to get the body off, but I couldn't get the glue off the fur and the whole thing was a mess."

I finished filling in the hole and took a seat under the willow tree. She was smart to pick this as the graveyard since the branches hid what was happening underneath the green sad leaves. It was the perfect place for sorrow.

"I think it's nice of you to care so much even if your parents don't." I said, watching her pat down the dirt followed by sprinkling grass clippings over the evidence. She thought of everything.

"Thanks. My mom said you moved in with your grandparents. Is that true?"

I didn't know how to answer that question; officially no one told me, unofficially, it's all the talk of the house. "I guess that's true."

"Then we will be friends." Roxy came and sat next to me. What was left of the sunlight flickered through the branches, making the sweat glisten on her summer-tanned skin.

The day Mom came home from what I overheard was a drug rehabilitation place, the house had been cleaned by Nan four times: twice the day before, and twice on that morning. She wanted to go with Pop to pick her up, but my aunt couldn't take off work and though Nan said it was no big deal, clearly it was and the only way to take her frustration out was with the vacuum.

The days that led up to the great and wonderful homecoming, we had many talks about what to expect, but what I concluded from all these conversations was that nobody had a clue. I was to be prepared that Mom may seem a little off and that I needed to give her time and have patience.

I wanted to tell them so badly that there was a large part of me that didn't want her to come back even if I missed her like the tides would miss the moon; but I felt guilty for even having those feelings and besides that, no one bothered to ask. Maybe that's because I tried to keep myself as little as a burden as possible and played with Roxy during the day and after dinner. I was used to making myself invisible, and I knew from experience that if you needed too much, then people would make it intolerable to be around. That was always the way it was with Mom, and if I ever mentioned I was bored or hungry, she would raise her voice to such a level that it felt like my head was going to come undone.

So instead of waiting for her like I was supposed to, I went out back and found Roxy. "You wanna take a walk?" I asked when I found her under the willow tree.

"What's the occasion?" She didn't bother looking up from the book she was reading, which was a loaner from the public library, her most cherished place.

"My mom is coming home today."

She finally broke her trance and looked up at me. Her green eyes seemed brighter after her recent visit to the Jersey shore. "Are you nervous?" She placed the book next her on the ground.

"I guess." I came over to her and sat down. "What are you reading?"

"This here is about butterflies. I murdered a caterpillar the other day and I felt so guilty that he never got to become a butterfly. I wanted to know how close he was to being able to fly, so I got this book out. Can you imagine? There he was inching along, just waiting to be free of the slow life and dirt and, splat, I came along. He was going to have wings, Tommy, and fly, and I took that away from him. Of all the creatures I try to save, I end up killing one of the most beautiful ones on the eve of his flight."

"How do you know he was about to fly?" I reached over her skinny legs and grabbed the book. "And how do you know it was a 'he'?"

"Technically, I don't know the answer to either of those questions, but I do know he would have flown soon. It's their life cycle."

I could hardly believe how long we sat under that willow tree hiding from the world, just waiting and holding our breaths. When Pop's car pulled in the driveway, my heart grew so tight, I thought I'd pass out.

"You gotta go." Roxy squeezed my hand and brought me back to life. "Come back outside if you can. I'll be waiting right here."

"See you later, alligator," I said.

"In a while, crocodile." She smiled at me and then resumed reading her book.

I snuck in the kitchen door, knowing that they came through the front door. I hadn't seen her in a month and when I left her last, she was hooked up to machines. They were in the living room. I could hear Nan crying and Mom whispering something. I turned back around, hoping to make it out of the house, but Pop stopped me dead in my tracks.

"You have to go in there and say hi, Tommy, it's the right thing to do." He threw his arm around my shoulders and guided me into the room.

There she sat like a bird on a branch waiting to take flight. She looked good at least; she seemed less tired and a bit heavier, but not by too much. I exhaled a heavy breath, finally knowing that she was still Mom and still here.

"Tommy," she said, and began to cry. I ran to her and threw myself into her arms. The universe was right again.

She made it three days. Then she was gone.

It had been a long time since I allowed myself to remember the day I woke up and found Mom gone. I opened her bedroom door like I had done the three previous mornings and found her bed a mess of blankets and the window opened. Even though I knew she wouldn't be on the other side of the window, I checked anyway, all the while my heart shredded open with agonizing pain. She had left us. She had left me. I walked the long, narrow hallway to my grandparents, knocked twice, and entered when they gave permission. I was hardly in my body; my mind was already racing for clues. Nan packed me up for school and gave me lunch money. I told Roxy on the bus through broken breaths that were not helping my oxygen-starved body. The other kids stared and whispered, but no one said a word to me. And as the hours went on in the school day, the hope began to build that she would be home when I came off the bus and that everything was going to be okay.

After the first couple months, the hope began to fade, and the routine of life kicked in like auto-pilot; but she always remained there, swimming around in my veins like blood coursing to the heart. Hope was never to be an anchor and sink to the sea floor; not even the strongest men in history denied hope. It was in the sunrise every morning.

DUKE

Dreaded math test, normally I hate you. Yesterday was the first test I took since working with Tommy. And he didn't take it easy on me the day before. He should be on payroll here with his mock tests and constant pacing like he's in front of a classroom full of students. All around the library desk, he circled me like a shark waiting to kill. The only expression on his face was frustration when I got the wrong answer. I thought about telling him he should throw a few compliments in for my self-esteem, but that made me feel even worse. I had to do better. Final answer.

Normally when I wait for the teacher to hand back our grades, I sit with a stomach full of boulders, but this time, there's something different. Its anxiety mixed with excitement because for the first time in my high school math career, I knew what the hell I was doing. And the high is better than I expected. Seeing that red penned A is just as good as seeing the end zone coming at me.

I let out a little cheer and my classmates quickly look my way. I lower my head to cover up my outburst because I don't want Mr. Todd saying something like, 'keep it down over there', in his teacher voice. I'm hanging this on the refrigerator next to all of Jayla's excellent grades. She has me beat in the academic department and the kicker is she's amazing at basketball, so I can't even walk around king of the world in the sports' department. But this A here will shut her up for a couple days. Bragging rights gone, Jayla.

Mr. Todd instructs us to start working from the next chapter while he organizes the things on his desk. There's the usual chatter among the class as we get our books open.

"What did you get?" Charlotte asks from the desk over.

"An A." I pass the paper to her even though we aren't friends or really know each other.

Well, I guess that's not true. I know of her because I've been in school with her since I can remember, but we've never had a reason to talk and this is the first class I've taken with her.

What I do know about her is that she hangs with the art kids. And I only know that because for a minute in ninth grade, Tim had a huge crush on Paige who is best friends with Charlotte. Of course, that didn't work out since Tim needed to talk sports and didn't understand anything revolving around art. The only thing he can draw is X's and O's and the reason he can do that is because of football. I think he still has a crush on her. There's just something hot about a girl out of your league.

"Damn!" She inspects the paper and passes it back. When I catch her eyes under the black frames of her glasses, I notice how green they are. Inviting.

"Not bad for the dumb jock." I give a quick laugh to cover up my buzz. Looking at this A has made it all worth it.

"Who said you are a jock?" She smiles back as she tucks her dirty-blond hair behind her ears.

I can't help but laugh. She reminds me of Tommy with the dry sense of humor. "What did you get?"

"I got a D." She pulls the sleeves down on her flannel shirt. "Dumb jock here looking for a sport to play. Not terribly gifted with the coordination part, but all heart."

"I heard cross-country isn't that bad," I offer.

"Ha! Maybe if I was being chased by a man with a machete."

"Oh, so it's gotta be a man doing the chasing. I see how it is with you."

"Women tend not to chase. They kill before they are finished with the sentence they are saying. You ever notice how your mom fights with your dad? Rapid fire integrations with accusations of crimes they may or may not have committed. Women are detectives with high caliber questions. Did you put that cup in the sink? Cause I saw you with that exact cup and now look at it in the sink. Do you know how many dishes I did today? You know, that kind of thing. So, to answer your question, yes it has to be a man doing the chasing because they have no clue how to use words as weapons."

"Touché, Charlotte."

"Charlie. I hate Charlotte. It sounds like an old person's name, or worse, *Charlotte's Web* and I hate spiders."

"Charlie is way better. Or maybe I'll just call you Grandma from now on."

"Funny."

"What did you say, Grandma?"

"Hahaha."

"But for real, maybe you can come with me to my tutor. That's my secret."

"And who is this brilliant tutor you speak so highly of? And how much money does it cost?"

"Tommy Moffe. And he doesn't charge, at least not for me."

"Tom Moffe talks?" She turns around at the sound of Mr. Todd's voice. Nobody dared to interrupt him.

As Mr. Todd continued with class, the buzzing in my stomach grew. This A represents so much more. I should ask Tommy to help me with the SATs. I can have more colleges wanting me.

The day went on as usual, but I remain on my high of being an A student. So high that when I see Kristy, I can't help but give her a bear hug and a kiss almost on the lips except that she's fighting me so it's more on the cheek.

"Get off me," she yells so loud that the hall goes quiet. "What is wrong with you, Duke?" The surprise in her eyes sobers me up. "I'm not interested in you. How many times do I have to tell you this?" She slaps my arm and storms away with the other cheerleaders surrounding her for protection. From me.

The heat from my cheeks is making me sweat. Everyone just saw and I can't say a word to defend myself. They all know the truth, but they look at me as if I just accosted her. Their whispers grow louder in my ears like a million bugs crawling all over my skin. I fight the urge to scream at them to shut up, the words building in my throat as they try not to look directly at me.

I speed walk to the gym, trying to make little eye contact with anyone. My phone buzzes with a new text. Kristy reminding me that her dad is best friends with the French teacher who happened to be in the hallway. Winky-face-heart emoji. I shove the phone back into my pocket.

"Hey, sexual predator," I hear Charlie's voice from behind me.

"Not funny."

"Too soon?"

"Yeah. It just happened."

"I have to say that was not your finest moment."

"What do you want?" I stop and turn directly towards her. I tower over her like a parent to a child. There's something in the way she cowers from me that scares me. "Sorry for yelling at you."

"It's cool. I get it, you're frustrated."

"You're kind of short," I say, stretching my arm straight so her head is below it.

"Or, and hear me out on this, you're kind of tall."

"No way. You're like a dwarf."

"You're like six-foot-three and I'm five-foot-five. I'm average and you're not."

"So, what I hear you saying is that I'm above average. Thank you." I breathe in deep, finally feeling my heart stop racing.

"If you put your above sized ego away for a minute, I was wondering if I could come with you and Tom. I don't want to fail Mr. Todd's class."

"You know I'm with Kristy, right? I didn't just grab her for no reason." I feel the need to justify what happened to her.

"Everyone knows, Duke. You guys are the modern-day Romeo and Juliet. So stinking cute except that you guys have to die and all. But besides that, more power to you."

"Shut up, Charlie." I loosen her backpack straps and watch as her bag droops down low.

"That about right. So, the tutoring thing?"

"I'll talk to him today."

"Thanks, and, hey, just so you know, I think they are filming *To Catch a Predator* in the area so you may want to keep your perv in check."

"Bye, Grandma."

"By, Dick, I mean Duke."

She cinches her backpack tight to her shoulders as she walks away. Her dirty-blonde hair sways back and forth with each step she takes, and it makes me smile again.

"Hey, Duke," she yells back down the hallway. "That wasn't cool what happened to you. You're a good guy."

Her words give me relief. If she said that, maybe other people think that too and not that I'm someone who goes around grabbing girls. I could get in serious trouble if people really thought that. Not to mention that Mom would ground me for life and probably disown me.

"Thank you, Granny," I yell. She disappears around the corner and I run to tutoring.

Tommy is less than thrilled when I tell him about Charlie. He has that faraway look; so distant that he could be in California and I could be here in New Jersey. I beg anyway. "It's for my friend," I say.

"Since when are you friends with Charlie? She isn't a cheerleader."

"I can have friends that are not football players or cheerleaders." I act hurt.

"Name one."

"Charlie."

"Name another one, Duke." He looks back at me, and I suddenly feel caged in. "That's what I thought," he says.

"Fine. Be that way. I happen to like her, and I figured you could help."

"What about Kristy?"

"No, man, I don't like her like that. I like her like she's funny and a friend, or could be a friend. Besides, I get her struggle in math. It's frustrating to barely pass."

"You're really racking up the B side of high schoolers. Lucky for you I think the B-side is always better."

"B sides?" I ask.

"B-side is a music reference. Never mind. Bring her tomorrow. But if she is distracting you, then she can't stay."

"Look who cares about me."

"Shut up, Duke, and open your textbook already. You're wasting my time." He cracks his awkward smile at me.

THE ORIGINAL WRECK: DISCOVERIES

TOMMY: AGE 10

I went to Six Flags Great Adventure with Roxy, her brother, and her father once. She wore hot-pink shorts and a baby blue PETA shirt that pissed her father off to no end. We were allowed to roam the park by ourselves because he was so infuriated. I'd never been on a roller coaster before and I was not really ready to find out if I made it out alive or not, but Roxy would not take no for an answer, and I didn't want to admit to being terrified. Isn't that how every hero's story starts? There's an obstacle, the protagonist doesn't really think they can overcome it, they do it anyway, and they win. It didn't occur to me that the protagonist would glue his eyes shut on the way up, beg for mercy, say out loud that he wanted to go home, squeal like a three-year-old on the way down, laugh when it was over, and then vomit while still fastened into the seat. But that's exactly how it went. She laughed at me, but her smile was more encouraging than mocking. She took my hand and ran to the next ride as if that experience never happened. She was my home. She made me safe in a world that was backwards and upside down all at the same time; she was the end of the ride, the brakes that slowed the cars to a steady stop.

Roxy's favorite ride was quickly becoming mine too for the sheer fact that it didn't take its time getting to the top. I realized after the third time that we rode it that what terrified me the most about the other rides was the long, slow crawl to the top. There was too much time to think about the ways you could die. And Roxy was not much help with all the talk about how high we were, and the daring feat of looking down, and last but not least, raise your hands above your head during the drop. But this particular coaster lifted you to the top fast, leaving you no time to think of ways to die.

"This time no hands at all," Roxy announced as she pulled her lap bar down. "No hands, Tommy." She studied my face. "You got this."

"I got this," I mumbled to myself, triple checking that the lap bar was secure before the train pulled away from the people who could help me.

"If you can do it, I'll buy you ice cream."

"Deal." I tapped the bar one last time and the ride took off. I fought the urge to pull my hands down the entire way up, but Roxy had her eyes glued to me so I couldn't cheat.

"You're free like a bird, Tommy, fly." She reached her hand over to mine and locked on. We rode the rest of the ride like this, our bodies bouncing from side to side in our seats.

"Ice cream on me," she said lowering her hands when the ride was over. "I can't believe you did it."

We made our way through the crowded park until we finally found the ice cream stand. It had been so many hours since I ate last.

"There you two are." Roxy's father appeared in front of us, his face as red as a tomato. "We're leaving now."

"We're about to get some ice cream, is that okay?" Roxy's voice was soft, which always surprised me even though that was the voice she used whenever she talked to her father.

"No, that's not okay. Do you see that line? Besides, your brother is already at the car waiting. I've been searching this whole park for you two for the last half hour. Now let's go." He grabbed her by her wrist and started walking away. I followed them a few steps behind. All around people laughed and raced to the next ride. The heat of the concrete play land we were on all day still swirled around us, mixed with the smells of cheese steaks and funnel cake. A lone water fountain stood, seemingly calling my name. My mouth was about as dry as the pavement I stood on, but I didn't want to lose Roxy and I was already having a hard time weaving in and out of people. By the time we reached the car, I was out of breath and confused as to what the rush was for anyway.

We rode in the back seat of her father's car mostly in silence. All around us the cars busied themselves speeding down the highway. Places to go. The sun set slowly, casting a pink sky that seemed endless if only it weren't for the rising moon. Her brother asked to stop for ice cream, but her father said, "I gave you enough today," and that ended any further discussions on the topic. Not that Roxy or I would chime in. We weren't his favorites even if he were capable of having such a thing, which he surely was not. And even though we were young, we were smart enough to know that he just took us to his company's summer event and that the ticket I used was Roxy's mother's, who never would have come in the first place. She hated crowds and waiting. "All that waiting," she said, "for a minute ride." When we pulled in the driveway, Roxy squeezed my hand so tight my skin tingled with a needle like sensation. She did this every time I left her like she wanted to desperately stay stuck to me. And I squeezed back like a call and response, I wanted to stay stuck too.

"Tomorrow," she said, "we go to the pool."

"Okay. I want a cannonball competition."

"So, you can lose again?" she asked.

"So, I can win."

"We'll see about that." She giggled and ran off to her house

"See you later, alligator," I hollered.

"In a while, crocodile."

I was up and ready in my swimming trunks by nine am even though the pool didn't open until noon. Nan was out in her garden talking to her plants. She was convinced that they could hear her and that they would respond to her loving words by producing a harvest to remember. Roxy, of course, loved this ritual, so it was never a surprise to see her wandering over to say a thing or two to the cucumbers, her favorite. Once I heard her say to the cucumbers that most people peel the skin of the cucumber off, but she had no intentions of separating what was rightfully supposed to be kept together. And then she gave that tiny plant a kiss and told it "I love you."

But that day, the day I waited in my bright orange swimsuit and no shirt, exposing my tanned skin and little muscles, my mother decided to come home. I heard the front door and should have been curious since Pop was supposed to be at work, but it went unnoticed as the huge event it would turn out to be.

It was only when she came barreling down the steps screaming that I knew she was back. After a year plus of missing someone, the natural thing would be to run to them. But her voice, her voice with the cackle of desperation and too many cigarettes came as a warning. Hide.

I scurried around the kitchen island, wanting something between us when she entered the kitchen. She appeared in the doorway. Pale. A bag of skin. Dark circles under her eyes. Her scrawny arms purple with fresh-looking puncture wounds. The sight of her startled me, my heart racing in pain from the missing and fear of seeing her. Really seeing her.

Did I never notice because this was how she looked every day we were together and there was some normalcy to it? Or was she worse than before? I couldn't decide. I wanted to ask, but all she wanted to do was yell for Nan, who came running.

"Where is my jewelry?" she demanded, rocking back and forth like she had to pee. "I need it. Now!"

"Sammy." Nan used a soothing voice like she was back out in the garden talking to the vegetables.

"Don't Sammy me, Mom. I'm not Tommy." It was the first time she acknowledged me.

"Can I get you something to eat? Here, sit down," Nan said.

"I'm not hungry. I'm just here for my stuff."

"Just a little something to eat. Maybe it will make you feel better." Nan walked to the refrigerator.

"Fuck, Mom. Just give me my shit," she said. Her body reminded me of electricity. Buzzing.

"Sam, I can't do that," she said. Her face broke like a fast-moving wave. First it was strong and rose high with might, and then it crashed down and turned to little droplets of tears.

"You're going to do it." She moved too close to me. I could feel her buzzing, a wanting for it to stop. A begging almost. I did what I thought was right. I hugged her to take some of the pain away.

"Get off me." She pushed my little body away and without warning, slapped me across the face. The stinging was like fire prickling the skin. But the shock was a whole damn grenade. A million little pieces of me shattered like fine china splintering into small, jagged splinters. All that hope, gone. Like a coward, I covered my face and hid my tears, finding shelter behind Nan.

"You need to leave." Nan's voice rose.

"Not without my stuff."

"Fine, then I'll call the cops."

"I'm not playing, Mom. Give it to me and I'll leave." She took a step toward us.

Nan took only one second to grab her phone from the counter and dial 911. She wasn't playing around either. But there were consequences for standing up to Mom. At first it was just whatever was on the kitchen island being thrown at us. The pepper shaker hit me square in the chest when Nan stepped away from me to stop her. But Mom continued around the kitchen, knocking over chairs and ripping pictures off the wall. She only stopped when she came across Nan's purse, from which she produced a tight, thin smile, and said, "This will do." She ripped the wallet out and ran out the back door.

When Roxy came over to find out why the police were at the house, my cheek was already swollen from the hand my mother laid on me. My eyes were red and burning from the crying. She squeezed my hand, and I squeezed back. Words would have only failed me. My mom, the monster.

DUKE

Jayla is in the kitchen when I finally make my way home from school. Practice ran a lot later than expected since Coach wanted to review some film. I can hear the television from the family room, "This is Jeopardy", drifts down the hallway. Larry loves watching this show with Mom and Dad. They are all very good and it's a highly competitive spectacle, which is why Jayla is probably hiding in here.

"Dinner is in the fridge," she says, looking up from her schoolbooks.

I open the refrigerator and pull out the plate Mom made me. Chicken and kale with a sweet potato. She prides herself on making me good lean meals. I heat it up in the microwave and begin working on making my protein shake.

"I hate the way that smells," Jayla says. "It's so gross."

I walk over to her and shake and shake the bottle, doing a little dance. "It's so good for you though."

I pull the top off and offer it to her.

"Get that out of my face! I'm going to puke." She pushes back her chair and stands into a long stretch.

Chugging the drink, I walk back to the microwave and patiently count down the seconds.

"By the way, your girlfriend not girlfriend is a real class act," she says, sitting back down. "Why do you let her talk to you like that? That's so embarrassing."

"It wasn't that bad." I rip my plate from the belly of the microwave at the sound of the first beep.

"Yes, it is. And the fact that you're not bothered by it is disturbing." She throws her pencil into her open notebook.

"It's not what it seems. I forgot her dad is friends with the teacher, so the optics looked bad. She reacted and cleaned it up. Not a big deal." I shove a giant fork load into my mouth so I don't have to speak.

"Duke, what's with this girl? You know how many other girls want to date you and you wouldn't have to lie about it? Is that part of it? You like the sneaking around?" Her face is serious. She reminds me of Mom when she gets like this.

"It's not really sneaking if the whole school knows." I take another big bite, this time trying to keep the words in my mouth. I don't want to fight. I don't want to have to explain.

"If the whole school knows, then so does the teacher and therefore, he will tell her father. A. B. C. Follow the bouncing ball, Duke. Something is not adding up and meanwhile she's embarrassing you in front of everybody."

"I'm not a dog, Jayla."

I take my plate, grab my school bag, and walk to my room. The jeopardy squad says hello as I pass by, but I'm not in the mood for small talk or listening to them yell at the television. Instead, I crash on my bed, balancing my food on my lap. I'm hungry, but not hungry. I'm so sick of defending Kristy to everyone when I know they would leave me alone if they knew the truth.

I pull my phone from my sweatpant pocket. Kristy has texted me ten times, and each one is getting more and more agitated. The first text was another sweet apology and the last one was a 'fine be that way', with the peace emoji. I take a chance and call her.

She picks up on the fifth ring. "What?" Her voice is sharp and to the point.

"I didn't feel like texting. Thought I'd change it up a bit and call."

"You've been changing it up a lot today. And thanks to you, my dad had a lot of questions about why you would behave that way toward me. I had to have an hour-long phone conversation with him. Stop being stupid."

I hang up without a goodbye, her voice digging into my ears. Stupid. She calls back, but I don't answer. I shouldn't have called in the first place. At least that's what all her texts are telling me as they come in faster than I can read. The last one says "You know the truth and you still don't care. We're done."

The last text hurts the most, but not more than the silence that follows. She's said all she had to. I put my plate on my nightstand and turn the light off. The darkness fills me, packing all my wounds like gauze.

The night I found her it was raining. Another summer pool party at JR's house while his parents were at the shore. A low-key party not to draw attention from neighbors. I didn't drink because I knew my parents would still be awake and being grounded during summer wasn't worth some beers for one night. When the rain started, everyone went inside and decided to break out the vodka. Not being drunk around them had consequences like the fact that I found them super annoying. Plus, I was tired from football camp and not juiced up from booze. Sleep was calling my name.

I left without saying goodbye. Cut through the backyard and almost hopped the fence. That's when I heard her. The sound of someone vomiting was dangerously close, like almost-step-in-the-pile-of-puke close. The smell stopped me cold.

"I'm sorry," she said, bent over in a praying position. Knees planted in the ground, back arched over, hair spilling all around her like a waterfall.

"Kristy?" I said quietly.

"I'm sorry. Did I get it on you?" She leaned up to look at me. Big chunks of vomit tangled in her hair.

"It's okay, Kristy. I'll take you home." I picked her up by her tiny waist. She felt light as a doll in my arms.

"No! I can't go home. My dad will kill me. Duke, I can't go home yet." The panic in her voice rose steadily.

"Okay, okay," I said, taking her hand. "At least let me take you back inside. You're soaking wet."

"Okay, Duke."

She wrapped her tiny hand around mine as I led her back to the house. Inside, the party was going even stronger. Shot glasses lined the kitchen table, with JR pouring sloppily everywhere. No one even noticed us pass by the room.

Upstairs in the quiet hallway, I led her to the bathroom and sat her on the floor. On the sink, I found a glass next to the toothbrushes. This house was big, at least double my home. But even with the size difference and all the newest and niceness of this house, it was run almost identical to mine. Kind of funny for how much we all try to think we are authentic in the end we are practically the same. Really, we all have to eat, shit, and brush our teeth. We all have to hang clothes and take showers. It's just done in a different shaped box.

I left Kristy hugging the toilet even though she hadn't thrown up. She said she liked the coolness of porcelain against her skin. I went to JR's room and found sweatpants and a hoodie piled up on his desk chair and went back to the bathroom.

"So, I can't put you in the shower for obvious reasons. I'm just going to wipe your face and hair down." I took the towel and wet it in the shower spigot and began wiping her face.

"Thank you." She grabbed my hand that was resting on her cheek. "I miss her, you know?"

Of course, we all knew Kristy's mom died a few years ago. We knew she was sick, and we knew when Kristy didn't come to school for a week and when she returned, she was always red-eyed from crying and that was how it went for the next few months until school let out.

"And the thing is, my dad doesn't talk about her anymore. We used to talk about her all the time. He used to tell me how much I look like her, and now he never talks about her. He talks about the new kids and the new wife and his new life. I don't belong."

"I'm sure it's not like that." We locked eyes and to me, it seemed like her eyes were begging to be seen. Sad and beautiful.

"It's like that. The twins rule the house. I'm just a glorified babysitter they call sister. And as long as I follow the rules, no one bothers with me. But when I break them, Duke, when I break them, then I'm the worst person in the world. I'm heading for Hell and a terrible influence on two-year-olds. Two-year-olds!"

I watched her cry as I continued to wipe her clean. I couldn't imagine my mother dying and leaving me here without her. All I wanted to do was hug Kirsty, but I didn't want to cross a line.

"I miss her so much. She would have loved me being cheer captain. She would have understood what a big deal it is. She would have told me not to date Cooper. So much for a church boy. He dumped me the day after I had sex with him." She was consumed by her tears, as if they were choking her inside out.

"That's messed up. Not all guys are like that," I said, toweling out the chunks of vomit from her hair.

"You're not like that." She said, taking both her hands and cupping my face. "You wouldn't hurt a girl. You wouldn't crush her just because you could."

"No. I wouldn't." Her mouth was close to mine. I could smell the liquor seeping off her breath. Still, it was hard not to kiss her. She was devastatingly beautiful. No makeup left on her face, tears still rolling down her cheeks, and her hair matted and tangled. She was the most elegant woman I'd ever seen.

"I don't know how not to be so sad. It's like a disease that has crawled up into my body and won't leave. No matter what I try to do, it just gets worse and worse."

"You got me now. You don't have to be so sad anymore. I'm not going anywhere."

She wrapped her arms around me and sobbed until she cried herself out of tears. I left her to change into the clean clothes. When she emerged from the bathroom ten minutes later, she looked like she intentionally came to the party wearing that outfit.

She wanted to go home and sleep in her own bed. I questioned her on judgement because I didn't want her to get caught, but she explained that her room was on the first floor of the house and all we needed to do was get her through her unlocked window. The air was still and humid after the rain, smelling of dirt and summer. We walked quietly down the shadowy streets, her hand tucked in mine. I hoisted her up so she could climb into her house that stood dark against the black sky. She slipped through her bedroom window like a burglar, and I knew she was safe when she turned her light on like we planned.

I promised her. She had me. Always. No more sadness.

I pick my cell phone back up, the glow from the screen burns my eyes a little. I text Kristy back. Sorry. Please don't be like this. I don't want this to end between us. Ever.

She takes a long time to write back. Bubbles appear to tell me she's typing but then disappear. Finally, she writes, me neither. Sorry too.

I close my eyes and fade back into the blackness.

THE ORIGINAL WRECK: BIRTHDAY TO REMEMBER

TOMMY: AGE 11

Late into August, the heat had scorched the grass to a rough, crunchy brown. Long gone was the soft grass of spring that held promise of warm weather and summer around the bend. The burnt grass was a daily reminder that fall was heading our way and with that, the return of school and schedules. With only a week left to go, everything felt like it was slipping away from us, which was why Roxy begged and begged her parents to let us camp out in the backyard. This was not new; she had begged all summer and her father said no every time.

My house had been unsettled since Mom came. "Things can be replaced," Nan said, as she canceled all her credit cards and bank accounts. But I heard it in her words. The same melancholy voice as mine. We witnessed an unraveling, and the little threads of Mom stuck to us like lint. There was no going back and no moving forward; there was only protection from her in the form of a home security system Pop had installed. "Just in case," he said.

Pop wanted to fix it. All of it. But he knew he could only do so much. So, for my birthday celebration, he somehow convinced Roxy's parents to let her sleep out in a tent in our backyard. Who knows how Pop pulled off that miracle, but to me it was just about the best birthday gift I could ask for shy of space camp.

There in the backyard stood an erect red tent, a fire pit, and skewers for s'more making festivities. For dinner, Nan made my favorite meal" homemade mac and cheese with cut-up hot dogs mixed in, which we ate inside so the bugs wouldn't stick to the noodles.

After dinner, Roxy pulled a perfectly wrapped gift out of her overnight bag. The wrapping paper was a brown paper bag which she drew all over, making it look more colorful than anything I'd ever seen on wrapping paper. It reminded me of a mural on a city wall. All little cartoons of us and the summer adventures we had, including the swim club, the library, the garden, and our adventures at the park on the roller coasters. The best one was me standing next to a ride with a puddle on the ground and tears in my eyes. Everyone took turns reading them before I carefully opened the present.

A baby blue PETA shirt to match the one she wore all the time.

"Happy birthday, best friend!" she yelled as I held up the shirt.

"I love it!" I pulled it over my head, impatiently jamming my arms into the sleeves. I wanted to know how she could have possibly gotten yet another PETA shirt past her father but felt it best to not question the amazing gift.

Pop excused himself and went to the other room while we cleaned up. When he came back, he held a large box with a red bow in his hands.

"Happy birthday!" he said and rested the box on the table. "Open this up, already."

I pulled the cardboard apart until the box revealed its contents. A shiny, blue acoustic guitar.

"Holy crap!" I said.

"Language," Nan reminded me.

"We got you lessons too," Pop added.

"I've been wanting this for so long," I whispered in awe.

"We know," Nan said, laughing. "It was hardly a secret."

Roxy and I played with the guitar while Pop started the campfire out back. The instructions said it came tuned, but we sounded horrible. Just holding our fingers down on the strings was a real challenge.

"I'm so jealous. You'll have to teach me everything you learn."

"I will. We can start a band."

"The PETA's," she said, smiling.

"Yes!"

"Come on, guys, the fire is ready," Pop yelled in from the back door. That was all we needed to hear to stop the planning of our band for the night.

That night, the humidity was tolerable and didn't wear on you like a light jacket. Pop didn't place too many logs in the fire pit. He only put enough in to where the flames would crisp, or in Roxy's case, incinerate the marshmallows. There we sat on green camping folding chairs, sticky with s'mores covering our hands and face, and a mean case of the giggle snorts when we noticed marshmallow slime covering a new and unexpected body part. For instance, Pop somehow had it all over his left ear, a string of white gently blowing in the wind. And when he went to swipe it off, he somehow managed to get it on his forehead. We laughed and laughed at him trying to clean it off until finally he went inside to clean it up.

"This is the best idea I've ever had," Roxy proclaimed, her face golden by the light of the fire. "We should have been camping out here all summer. Maybe we can do it on the weekends. Until it gets too cold. And next summer we should build a tree fort. Not a little fort, I mean high off the ground with walls and a roof. And that's where we will write our songs. The PETA's are going to be famous!"

"Definitely. I think it will have to be in my yard. No way your dad says yes to that in his." I shoved an entire s'more in my mouth. My belly warmed from the goo. I watched as Nan came walking toward us from the house. She declined the invitation to sleep in the tent because she loves a comfy bed too much. In her hands, she held a couple bottles of water.

"I thought you could use these, or maybe I should turn the hose on and clean you up." She passed out the waters. We screamed no to the hose and laughed at her imitating how she'd spray us down, making sure not to get too close to catch a case of the marshmallows. Roxy threatened Nan with her arms stretched out long, everything nature stuck to her marshmallow fingers. I examined my own hands and wondered how the dirt got there since I hadn't touched anything. Turned out marshmallows are like tiny magnets with an incredible pull to suck anything to it.

"Listen to me," Nan said seriously as she sat in the vacant chair. "Pop is a heavy sleeper, so I want you to be alert in case you hear anything in the night. I was just on the phone with the neighborhood watch and they said that just north of us an inmate escaped and is on the loose. I'm sure it's nothing but just be mindful."

"What?" Roxy sat up straight in her chair next to me. "What do you mean be mindful? Should we not sleep at all? Or sleep with a skewer by our side?"

"No. No. I didn't mean to upset you. Just, if you hear anything, wake Pop up, that's all."

"Maybe we shouldn't sleep outside at all," Roxy said. "We could sleep inside in the family room. That seems safer."

"Everything is fine. Don't worry about it," Nan said. She sat still on her chair as if she was wondering if sleeping inside wouldn't be a bad option. "I'm sure they'll catch him soon if he hasn't already been caught."

"Maybe we should go inside now," I chimed in, the sugar high suddenly crashing down on me. "Roxy's right, the family room is just like a tent but with walls that are secure."

"Don't be silly." Nan stood. "I'm getting chewed alive out here by the mosquitoes." She slapped her arm and began to walk away, but suddenly stopped.

"Did you hear that?" she asked us.

"Hear what?" I replied.

"That!" she whispered.

Behind our chairs, the sound of twigs breaking rang out in the blackness of the night. Suddenly, it was too dark. Too late. Too outside unprotected by walls. Then the crunching stopped.

"Maybe you guys should get up," Nan whispered. "Nice and slow."

Roxy and I sat frozen in our chairs. She whispered to me that we needed to get up on three. We shifted our bodies in the seats, but it was too late.

I felt the hand grab my shoulder with a death grip. I turned and looked to find the grim reaper holding us down. I yelled out "no" and tried to reach for Roxy. She threw her water on me. The grim reaper snorted with laughter and then ripped the mask off. Pop.

"Pop!" I yelled. "That wasn't funny." My heart was racing, and my legs were shaking with utter terror.

"That was the best thing ever!" Roxy shouted out into the night sky.

"You two should have seen your faces!" Nan wailed in laughter. "Priceless."

"So funny, hahahaha," I hollered at her.

After the commotion settled down, we went inside to clean ourselves off and change into our jams. I was nowhere near tired. Roxy came out of the bathroom wearing a *My Little Pony* tank top and pink shorts. Under her armpit on the inside of her arm I saw it. A bruise that looked identical to fingers. Large fingers. She noticed me looking but walked away.

Pop fell asleep right away. Roxy was giving him the play-by-play of how she thought the first day of school was going to go and somewhere between Ella from two blocks over bragging about her summer at camp and our new teacher Mrs. D, Pop decided to check out for the night. Of course, Roxy didn't care and continued.

"Hey," I interrupted. "How did you get that bruise?"

"What?" she asked.

"The bruise on your arm. It looks like fingers."

"Oh that."

"Yeah, that."

"It's nothing, Tommy." She rolled over in her sleeping bag, which sounded like she was stuck in a silk trap. I let her silence settle in between us. Pop's heavy snores filled the tent.

"But it's not nothing. It's something," I finally said.

"I found another mouse on the glue trap. I took my dad's work gloves and got them stuck. He got mad and grabbed me by the arm. No big deal." She moved again, and I imagined her like a silkworm.

"Okay."

"Night, Tommy."

"Night, Roxy."

"Best night ever!" I could hear the smile in her voice. "See you later, alligator."

"In a while, crocodile."

It wasn't a big deal. He just grabbed her too hard. That could happen. I closed my eyes and listened over the snoring to the crickets that filled the night. Their own private orchestra uninterrupted while the humans slept. I felt her hand grab onto mine. She gave a little squeeze, and I squeezed back.

DUKE

I keep my distance from Kristy all day because she asked me to and because it felt like everyone was watching me after yesterday's performance. I watch her laugh her easy laugh with a smile so wide it could draw in anyone close enough to its gravitational pull. She's airy in her movements, light as a feather. I'm heavy like a Brachiosaurus, limbs crashing against the linoleum floors, my entire mass too big for this tiny space. I can't seem to shake the hollow feeling every time she sneaks a peek at me. That used to be exciting, this secret we shared. The knowing. But today it leaves me cold.

"Hey, perv," Charlie said, walking up to my locker. "Thanks again for getting Tom to tutor me." She leans against the locker next me; her backpack looks like an overstuffed turtle shell.

"No problem." I close my locker and slap the lock back on it.

"What's with you?" she asks.

"What do you mean?"

"You just seem off. Didn't even yell at me for calling you a perv."

"Nothing is wrong with me." I start walking.

"Oh no, is my little perv sad?" She squeezes my arm. "Sad little guy, why're you so sad? Little Bo Peep lost his sheep." She laughs at herself.

"First off, Little Bo Peep is a girl."

"Oh, why's it gotta be a girl? Now who's sexist?"

"Little Bo Peep is a girl because that's what it says in the rhyme." I pick up my step to match her almost bounce/walk.

"Okay, fine, that seems like a good enough answer."

"You are the most annoying person I've ever met." I give her a little push on her arm.

"Not even five minutes together and you're trying to perv me up." Her smile catches me on fire.

"You haven't lived if you think arm touching is pervy."

"Says the perv."

We bounce/walk the rest of the way to the cafeteria to meet Tommy. He insisted that we meet here instead of the library because he didn't think we could be quiet enough for the librarian's liking. He's probably right since I think she would prefer it if we used sign language or hieroglyphic drawings to communicate.

When we walk into the cafeteria, there are other groups of students sitting at tables. At the far end, I spot Tommy.

He sits at the table like a statue, seemingly encased in sadness for eternity. When he does notice us, only a tiny smile appears at the edges of his mouth.

"Charlie this is Tommy, Tommy this is Charlie," I say, trying to break up the uncomfortable energy floating around us. He looks at me with disdain.

"I know who Charlie is, Duke." Tommy cracks open his math book. Charlie gives me a sideways look as if surprised that Tommy did know her. "This should be easy," he continues, "since you guys are in the same class. Charlie, what's your grade in there?"

"Solid F, but not without effort. I really do try. I just don't understand it." She looks away from Tommy and pulls at her sleeves.

"Cool. As long as you're trying, this shouldn't be too hard."

Tommy geeks out with the math lesson for an hour before I have to call it quits to get to practice.

"Tom, you're the best explainer of math that I have ever met," Charlie says, starting to pack up her things. "I have to get to work."

"Where do you work?" Tommy finally asks a personal question. I drop my pencil on my notebook in disgust. Dude has never asked me a personal question.

"The Coffee House. I make a mean coffee; like if coffee was soft like Batman then I'd be the Joker." She laughs at herself. "I got to get moving because I have to walk there."

"I'll give you a ride. It's on my way home. And since when is Batman soft?" Tommy says.

"Since he plays dress up and wears a cape."

"That's his armor," Tommy protests.

"And the cape is for what? Glamor is the obvious answer."

"It's so he can glide. Have you seen the movies?"

"I get it. I touched a nerve," she says. Her smile is infectious because he is smiling back. "Now about that ride, Batman."

Jamming my books in my bag, I tower over the table as they work out the details. There's a little burn of resentment that they get to leave together and go home.

"Later, freaks," I say.

The locker room is all mine as I change into my practice gear. I can hear Joe the PT trainer moving around in his office. The buzz of a text message coming across my phone makes me jump.

I see that it's a message from my mom, but ignore it and run out to the field. Coach beats the crap out of us, pushing us harder than he ever has. I taste the vomit rising from my stomach during wind sprints and almost heave when Smookler tosses his cookies.

By the time we get back to the locker room, I am drenched in sweat and dog tired. It isn't until I'm walking to Tim's car that I check my texts and see one from Jayla. I open it. My whole world stops. The picture blurs as my eyes try to adjust and refocus on what I'm actually seeing. But there is Kristy kissing Wyatt Davis clear as day. Jayla simply wrote: she's playing with you.

I text her back and ask where this picture was taken. I can hear Tim talking to me, but I can't move. Not until Jayla writes back.

Tim comes and stands next to me and sees what I'm staring at. "Is that Kristy and Wyatt?"

"Fuck," I scream. I want to smash my phone against the blacktop, but Jayla finally answers.

Food court at the mall twenty minutes ago. Bitch.

I quickly copy the photo and send it to Kristy. No words attached. I begin to walk to the passenger side door.

"Want to go to the mall?" Tim asks as he starts the car.

"No," I answer, but every part of me wants to go to the mall. I want to beat the shit out of Wyatt. I want to scream at Kristy until this razor I just swallowed cuts me whole. But I know I can't do any of that because of football.

When he parks his car in front of my house, he asks again if I want to go find them. "Shit's not right. We can go yell at him. We can't get in trouble for yelling."

"It's not worth it," I say.

"You're better off without her."

"Yeah," I say, opening the door to get out. "Thanks."

I go straight to my room when I get home and lay on my bed, staring at the picture. Memorizing every last detail down to the way his hips are angled into hers. Her hand gently rests on his chest as his lips are perched half open on the side of her mouth. Aren't they a great looking couple?

"Knock knock." Jayla opens my bedroom door.

"I don't want to talk about it." My words are short, the anger at a boiling temperature.

"I'm not here to talk. Just running some interference with the parents. I told them I'd bring you dinner so you don't have to talk to them."

"Thanks." I exhale deeply and feel the tears building.

"You okay?" She slides the dinner plate onto my desk.

"No."

"If you need me, come get me." She leaves and gently shuts the door. She really is the best sister.

It seems like years passed waiting for Kristy to text back. And when she does finally respond it just says it's not what it seems.

I don't wait for another text and call her because I don't care if she gets in trouble and is grounded for the rest of her life. She deserves that and so much more. Actually, what she deserves is me showing up at her house and making a scene so her father knows without a doubt we were together.

"Why are you calling?" she screams into the phone.

"What the hell is wrong with you? Why do you think I'm calling? Why were you kissing Wyatt?"

"First of all, I need you to calm down and stop yelling at me. Can you do that?"

I'm silent out of shock, not out of obedience, but she takes it like I'm willing to obey her.

"Okay then, I've been meaning to talk to you all day but didn't want to risk it. My dad suggested last night during our talk that Wyatt likes me and that, as you know, he's from the church, so that would make my dad very happy. I talked to Wyatt, and he agreed to help me because he likes you. So, Wyatt is our buffer. I fixed the problem that you created."

"You expect me to believe that?" I answer after a long pause.

"Check your texts," she answers.

I look at the app and wait as pictures of texts messages appear from Kristy. One after the other, the conversation she and Wyatt had about this fake kiss populates the thread.

"Duke, I'm sorry I didn't tell you. You had that tutoring thing after school then football, and I ran into Wyatt at the mall. So, we just decided to get it over with."

I let the silence settle between us as I fact checked reality. Read and reread the texts and examined the photo until I could envision it clearly with my eyes closed.

"Duke, I know you're mad, but I did this for us. I love you. And I want nothing to get between us."

"Wait. Go back to what you just said." My heart still feels like shrapnel tore into it, but then there were those words. Three little words.

"I love you," she says so low it is almost a whisper. "You know that."

And now my heart is dancing to a wild and crazy rhythm pounding out of my chest. "I love you, too."

"I got to go before I get caught. Talk to you tomorrow. I love you."

"I love you too." I say it again. I can't fight the smile. I let that smile take my whole face over and it feels good. She loves me.

So, what if no one understood us? We do. And that's all that matters. No one else is in this relationship with us.

THE ORIGINAL WRECK: ACCIDENTS

TOMMY: AGE 12

When my grandparents got the call, I was the one they forgot. I was out at the library with Roxy which was now our favorite place to do homework. We had permission to leave after school and walk there, and one of my grandparents would pick us up. To Roxy, she said, it felt like an escape. She claimed her brother would harass her at home and her mother would do nothing. Roxy picked the library over my house for the sheer fact of geography. If we were at my house, it felt like the tentacles of her house could easily reach out and suction cup her back to hell.

We had a nice little routine of knocking out our homework and then studying all the books we could find on how to play the guitar. On this night we decided to work on our lyrics notebook instead. We'd been collecting our favorite music lyrics in order to try and break them down and understand what makes a good song good. It wasn't a simple task. There were verses and bridges, and you couldn't fill the spaces with useless words. They had to mean something. Every note. Every word.

When it was time to get picked up, we packed up and waited by the entrance of the lobby. The late April weather had been hit or miss the last couple of days, but on this night, it was warm in the sun.

We waited and waited.

"I think your grandparents forgot us," Roxy said, kicking the half wall I was sitting on.

"It is strange. I'll call again. Maybe they are out shopping or something." I rang the house line and their cell phones, all the while a tight little rock formed in my chest. They never forgot to pick us up before.

"Let's just start walking, Tommy."

"But then they won't see us when they get here."

"Maybe something is wrong." She looked at me, her eyes full of concern.

"Yeah, okay, we should start walking."

We walked all the way home in silence, which took about an hour. I couldn't imagine a scenario in which they could simply leave us to walk this far alone. Nan's car was still in the driveway, but Pop's was gone.

"I'll come in with you." She followed behind me to the front door, which was left unlocked. A fact that felt alarming given Pop's impeccable security practices of late.

"Nan?" I yelled.

The house answered back with complete silence. We checked every room until we were convinced the house was empty.

"I have to go home before I get in trouble. Want to come with me?"

"I'm going to stay in case they come home."

"If you change your mind come over." She gave me a look over and left. "See you later, alligator." Her words are almost more a question than a statement.

"In a while, crocodile."

I didn't bother turning the television on. I sat in the family room staring at my phone, willing somebody to call me. I nearly jumped out of my skin when the front door opened.

"Just me," Roxy said. She held a plate of food in her hands. "My mom sent this and wanted to know if anyone has called. She also said you can't stay here alone tonight. You have to sleep over if no one comes home. She also called the hospital and neither of your grandparents are patients, so that's good news."

"That is good news." I let out the breath I'd been holding.

"It's just baked chicken, but it's pretty good," Roxy said, putting the plate on my lap. She picked up the remote control and turned the television on.

An hour later, the front door opened again, this time scaring both of us.

"Pop!" I jumped from my seat.

"Roxy, it's time for you to go home," Pop said, his voice so thin I could barely hear him. I took the sight of him in. His puffy eyes and tired walk made me anxious. Roxy, who was one for talking, took one look at him and headed for the door.

Pop took a seat next to where I stood. "Sit down, Tommy."

But somewhere in me knew what he was going to say. Deep down in my tissues, I already knew something was missing.

"It's your mom."

A narrative I knew could play out because I'd seen it so many times before on television shows and movies. A drug overdose. A parentless child. I was no fool thinking that this couldn't be my life since I was living some kind of tragedy anyway. But this news, this news was like a bullet from a sniper high on a roof top. It pierced me fast.

"Tommy, your mom." He stopped speaking. His face went from hard to sagging in a moment's time.

"What happened? A drug overdose?" I tried to guess what his next words would be.

"No. No. A car accident." His tears slid silently down his cheeks. "She was clean. Five months. Her longest. She didn't want to tell you because she thought if she slipped it would devastate you. She wanted to be clean at least six months. She wanted to make sure she didn't let you down again."

"Car accident," I said.

"She was driving home from work in the group van and someone ran a red light. She didn't have her seatbelt on. The impact from the crash left her brain dead. I know this is all coming at you fast, Tommy, but I need to know if you want to see her before we make the final decision of taking her off life support."

"I want to see her," I said. Those five words broke me.

"I'm so sorry, Tommy." He grabbed onto me, his hug nearly crushing me.

We drove in silence to the hospital a half hour away. She was trying to remain sober. Five months. There wasn't a memory I had where she wasn't wrestling with addiction. I would have liked to see her sober.

When we came through the wing of the hospital, it was as if all the staff knew I was there to say goodbye. They couldn't hide their faces fast enough in the bright, white hallways. We entered the last room on the left. Nan and my aunt sat beside Mom, holding her hands. When they saw me, they cried loud, painful cries that hurt deep down inside of me.

I walked to her bed. A breathing tube was shoved down her mouth. They cleaned up most of the abrasions on her face and covered what Pop told me was her head injury that left her brain dead.

I touched her hand, still warm with life. The last time I saw her, she was stealing money. The last time I thought about her was so many months ago I couldn't remember. But here she was. All I ever wanted. Clean. Sober. And I'd never get to see what we could have been like. Mother and son.

The doctor explained that they would wheel her into the operating room, and they would unplug the machine. She would eventually stop breathing and once that happened, the hospital staff, himself included, would step in to harvest her organs since she was a donor. The family, of course, would be ushered out of the room before that happened.

"Tommy, I don't think you should be a part of this." Nan spoke up.

"I'm coming. She decided that she wouldn't see me until she was six months clean and I'm deciding that I'm going in that room."

"I'm not really comfortable with this. You're going to stay out here," she continued as if I didn't say anything.

"Let him go," Pop spoke. "It's his right to say goodbye. We don't get to take that from him."

Nan went to argue but changed her mind.

They took Mom first and then led us into the operating room. The lights were dimmed except just above the table that she laid on. The doctor and his staff stood against the wall in the darkness like shadows. We surrounded the table and touched her as someone gave us the step-by-step of what was about to happen.

"When you are ready, we will turn the equipment off," the person said.

"How will we ever be ready?" Nan asked and then bent and hugged Mom. "I'm not ready."

Pop leaned over her, stroking her back and whispering in her ear that it was time. Nan wailed. Her sorrow drowned every inch of me.

I leaned over and kissed Mom's face. "I'm sorry for hating you so much," I said, choking on my tears. "I love you. I think you can still hear me, Mom. I love you," I whispered in her ear.

"We're ready," Pop said.

I didn't look up, but I heard the machine stop. The room fell quiet. Just the sound of our tears and her heartbeat machine filling the walls. I knew the flatline beat was approaching with how distant the beeps were becoming. I told her I loved her one last time before the resting line. We were removed quickly.

Things were said in the hallway to my grandparents, but I couldn't listen anymore. She was gone, and what could they say that I would find useful? I was too consumed with disgust to care. I hated myself for hating her. Hated that she lived a life for her instead of me. And then when she tried, she died anyway.

On the way back home, my grandparents told me they would be arranging for her to be cremated and they would not be holding a service for her because she would have protested that, and they wanted to do what they thought she would want. That was what they felt best. I felt nothing.

I slept in bed with them that night. I didn't care that I was too old for that sort of thing. I couldn't be alone in my room.

Roxy came over the next morning in her pajamas even though it was a school day.

"My mom said I could stay home with you." She gave me a giant hug and let me cry on her for what felt like an hour. We watched television for the rest of the day as my grandparents roamed the house like zombies. Periodically, Roxy would squeeze my hand and I would squeeze back.

Greif allows no room for forgiveness. It just takes you whole and wraps you tight like a swaddled newborn baby. Grief blankets you with missed futures and words you can never say again to the person. It only leaves you empty yet full of regret.

DUKE

The Wyatt plan, as Kristy and I now call it, has many great benefits like the fact that we can talk on the phone since her dad thinks it's Wyatt. But the most important one is that now Kristy has an excuse to be out after cheer and can drive me home from football practice.

"You sure you don't want a ride?" Tim says as he grabs his bag off the bench in the locker room.

"I'm good." I check my cell phone, nervous that our plans have changed, but Kristy texted saying she's ready. I hurry up and grab my bag and head for the front of the building where she is parked, waiting for me.

"Hey stranger," She says as I scoot into the passenger seat. She leans in and gives me a long kiss.

"It's so good to see you," I say, buckling my seatbelt.

"Will your parents miss you if I don't take you right home?"

"No. Where should we go?"

"Don't you worry about it." She grabs my hand and locks her fingers in between mine.

She pulls out onto the main street and heads the opposite way of my house. Ten minutes later, we end up at a little park we all used to play in growing up.

"Kemper Park?" I ask. "It's kind of dark, you know?"

"Is Duke afraid of the dark?"

"No. More like afraid of getting in trouble."

"I promise no trouble, now follow me." She hops out of the van and opens the side door, grabbing a bag out of the seat. I walk next to her as we head into the mouth of the park. She abruptly stops and drops the bag. She pulls out a blanket and spreads it out over the grass.

"Have a seat," she says, pulling out the fake candles that you switch on. "We're having a picnic."

"Really?" I say, pulling her body into mine and giving her a kiss. "Right here in the dark?"

"Right here in the dark."

I lower our bodies to the blanket. We are tangled together, legs weaved through each other's, arms wrapped around our bodies. I am somewhere between the hard earth and heaven as she kisses me hard and then soft. Our breath heavy with need.

"Wait," she says and backs away from me. "I can't sleep with you. Not yet. I'm not ready."

"That's not what I was expecting, Kristy." I give her a kiss on the cheek.

"I love you, Duke."

"I love you, too." I take her hand in mine. "Don't ever feel like you have to do that with me. I mean, if you want to that's cool, I just don't want you to feel pressured." I kiss her hand.

"Here." She pulls a sandwich from her bag. "Your favorite, turkey and cheese. I got one too."

We sit on the blanket in the dark, eating the best turkey sandwiches I've ever had.

"How's the tutoring going?" she asks.

"Good. I've got my grade up to a solid B. I don't know what I'd do without him. He's like a genius who knows how to teach. I'd be screwed without him. There's a lot of recruiters coming and talking to Coach about me. Have you started applying to colleges? We should go to the same school."

"I just finished my essay. I really want to go far away, but my dad gave me a budget and told me that if I pick too far, I can only come home for the major holidays. Fine by me. But my budget is kind of tight unless I get a cheer scholarship."

"What are the chances of that?" I asked.

"Right now, it's looking pretty good for some schools in Pennsylvania."

"That's not far. I've got a couple schools there on my list. I need a scholarship too. Money is kind of tight at my house, not that my parents talk about it too much, but my dad has made some comments about hoping I get some money. I'm really hoping to get into Temple University."

"I'll apply there too then." She leans over and kisses me.

We laid on the blanket for a while with the chilly fall air blowing around us. If it wasn't for the rain, maybe we would have stayed all night.

When she pulls up to my house, I feel the sudden pain of missing her. "Hey, about the dance this Friday after the game."

"I have to go with Wyatt. Keep the lie going." She leans over and gives me a peck. "I know it's a big night for you. Player of the year award."

"It's okay," I lie. "See you tomorrow."

We win the game by a landslide and clinch the playoff spot. After the locker pep talk, we shower and head to the dance. I'm all butterflies because right after the game I was awarded player of the year that came with a scholarship of five hundred dollars and an interview with the local paper.

My dad's face was priceless. For such a tough man, he sure can produce a lot of tears. I am practically floating into the gymnasium. The dance was already in full swing as the football team came in.

"Duke!" Some of my classmates cheered.

I made my way over to the food table and loaded up on soft pretzels and cheese.

"I don't know how you put up with that shit," Smookler says.

"What shit?" I ask, piling chips on my plate.

"Kristy and Wyatt." He looks at me as if I am dumb.

"It's her cover."

"That's one hell of a cover." He spins my body around so I have a full view of Kristy making out with Wyatt on the dance floor.

Nothing has prepared me for this moment. The anger starts from my stomach and penetrates out through my limbs. I need to punch something or someone. I need to scream. This wasn't a part of the deal.

"Part of the plan," I say, trying to keep my cool.

I drop my plate in the trash and head out of the gym. By the time Charlie finds me, I'm pacing back and forth outside under the streetlight.

"Hey, Duke," she says, coming up to me.

"What the fuck?" I scream. "This wasn't part of the plan. She's in there making me look like an idiot. I had the biggest night of my life and she's in there practically fucking Wyatt."

"Congrats on tonight. I mean I know right now you're not feeling great, but that's awesome that you won that." She is pacing next to me. "Did you see Tom came? He never comes to school shit, but I saw him there and he said he wanted to see you win the award. That's pretty cool."

"Why would she kiss him? Really? Why?"

"I don't know the answer to that."

We pace in silence for a while.

"I hate her," I say and feel the tears I've been holding in finally slip out. "I fucking hate you," I shout into the night.

"Okay. Well, I think it's time we get out of here." She grabs my arm and pulls me to her car.

"I think I should go back in. I think I should say something to her."

"No, Duke. That's just about the stupidest thing I've heard you say and last week you struggled with adding seven plus five."

"I was really hungry that day. Tell me why I shouldn't march in there and say something to her face?"

"Because that's what she wants you to do."

"What?"

"She's all about attention, Duke. All eyes on me. And if you go in there and get in trouble, what does that prove? That you love her?"

"Maybe. Or maybe she'll know I'm done with her."

"Silly boy, you're not even close to being done with her. Everyone knows that but you. Now I'm not about to let you get in trouble so get in my car or I will kick your ass."

I stop and look at Charlie for the first time all night. "Why do you care?"

"Because you got Tom to tutor me. You saved me from an F in math and kept my college dream alive. I owe you. I'm starving. Want to grab some fast food?"

"I want to go inside and make this right," I say, but open her car door instead.

"It's a lot cooler that you don't play into this."

We drive to the nearest fast food place and head inside. We order burgers, fries, and milkshakes.

"I got this," Charlie says, paying the cashier. "Celebration dinner for your big night."

We grab the closest booth and slide in.

She pops the lid off her chocolate milkshake and begins dipping her fries into it.

"Gross. What are you doing?"

"Don't knock it until you try it." She pushes the shake toward me.

"Fine but only one." I dip a warm fry into the shake and shove it in my mouth. "Holy shit! That's actually good."

"Told you so!" She gives me one of her huge Charlie smiles.

Halfway through the food, I start to feel better. Or at least less likely to punch a complete stranger.

"So, Tommy came? That bastard."

"Yeah, that weirdo does like you for some strange reason. He's actually kind of cool."

"Oh, someone's got a crush on Tommy. My man."

"No, I don't!" She laughs. "It's just a shame people don't know him because he's pretty funny. I don't understand why he doesn't like anyone. Not one single friend."

"That's not true. I'm his friend."

"You are such a dork." She throws a fry at me and it lands on my sweatshirt. I take my container, which is almost gone, and chuck it back at her.

"Dumbass!" She laughs wiping off the fries. "Now you have less to eat."

"Nope." I swipe her fries and dump them in my mouth. "Now you have less to eat," I say between bites.

By the time Charlie drops me off, Kristy is waiting for me in her parked car in front of my house.

"Sometimes it pays to be the one who gets chased. Remember that, Duke. See you Monday."

I get out of her car and watch as she pulls away.

"Duke," Kristy says, "where have you been?"

"Avoiding you."

"I'm so sorry. My dad was at the dance. I just wanted to make sure he believed Wyatt and me. I'm so sorry, Duke. I love you so much." She wraps her arms around my body and holds me tight. "Please, say something. I can't lose you."

"Don't ever do it again." I let her hug me. "I can't take much more of this."

"I'm so sorry."

"I've got to get inside." I give her a squeeze back and push her off me.

"Do you forgive me?"

"Yeah, I forgive you."

THE ORIGINAL WRECK: MERCY

TOMMY: AGE 12

My mother came to me every night in my dreams for the next several weeks. At first, she would just be in the background of the dream. For instance, I dreamt of chasing after the school bus and when it slowed and let me on, I would see Mom sitting in the back, a face among all the usual classmates.

But one night she came to me and sat on my bed and didn't speak. This went on and on, night after night, and I thought about telling my grandparents, but I didn't want to worry them. It wasn't long after Mom died that I overheard a conversation my aunt was having with them about me. I was supposed to be out with Roxy, but she had to go in early. My aunt sat perched on her kitchen chair, telling them that they needed to consider putting me in therapy and maybe having me live with her at least during the summers to give them a break.

Pop put an end to the conversation quickly, but since then I'd been feeling the need to be extra small and trouble free. The last thing I needed was to be taken from Roxy.

So, when Mom decided to talk to me in my dreams I decided to listen and not say a word to anyone. I grew fond of our little chats. She always said nice things to me. She always reminded me that she loved me and missed me. It was the first time in my life I didn't feel anxious of her presence.

But then that changed. She came to me angry and bleeding from her head wound. She cried and hollered that she would have never been in that car if it wasn't for me. She was living the life she wanted and gave it all up to get sober and sacrifice herself to her personal failure: me.

Night after night I woke up crying and sweating profusely. She was so real and so mean. And then she tried to choke me to death.

I woke up begging for help. Pops practically broke down my bedroom door trying to get to me.

"Tommy," he said. "Wake up. Wake all the way up."

"I'm awake," I cried.

"It's just a bad dream," he said, turning on the light by my bed. "Just a bad dream." He scooted his body next to mine.

"She's real in the dreams," I said between breaths.

"Mom?"

"Yeah," I said, my voice barely above a whisper.

"I know it feels like she's real."

I tried to calm myself down so he wouldn't worry, but it was hard to catch my breath, even harder to slow my racing heart.

"Look, Tommy, you haven't said much about her passing and maybe that's a problem. You need to let it out and talk to me and Nan."

"I can't."

"Why do you feel like you can't?"

"Because I don't want to be a problem. A problem is something you have to solve and what if the solution is sending me to Aunt Tammy's?" I closed my eyes, dreading to hear him confirm my fear.

"I would never send you to live with Aunt Tammy. Why would you think that?"

"I heard you guys talking and she said you guys needed a break."

"She was talking out her ass, Tommy. She's grieving, and she thinks Nan and I are old. But here's the thing, Nan and I are not too old to love you. And we love you so much. I would miss you too much to send you anywhere. You belong here with us. And we want to help you, so you need to start talking. You can't hold this in, and you don't have to face this alone."

"You promise you won't get rid of me?"

"Yes, Tommy, I promise."

"I promise too," Nan said as she came through the door.

"See? We both promise," Pop said.

"Just talk to us. Whatever you have to say, we love you." She handed me a glass of water.

"What was the dream about?" Pop asks.

"She was choking me to death. She said it was my fault she died. She said she hated me since the day I was born and wished I never saw the light of day."

"That is pretty scary," Pop said.

"I know we haven't really talked about what was going on with your mom before she died," Nan said, taking a seat in my desk chair. "She overdosed five months ago on a park bench in Philadelphia. The paramedics gave her Narcan and were able to save her life. The doctor at the emergency room told her that next time she would most likely die. Your mom asked for paper so she could write you a letter to say goodbye and apologize for letting you down. After she finished, she called us and told us she didn't want to die. She wanted to be in your life as your mom. Pop and I found a good treatment facility, but we knew the rest was up to her. She asked for us not to tell you."

"The thing is, Tommy, none of this is your fault and you shouldn't blame yourself," Pop said.

"I know she hated me," I said.

"She didn't hate you," Pop said. "It just probably felt that way because looking at you made her hate herself. Made her hate her decisions and the inability to change. Does that make sense? Because even if you didn't always feel it, she did love you very much."

"She made bad choices, Tommy, but she chose to keep you. She wanted to be sober for you. It may not have seemed like it, but she did. Even when she should have let you go, she tried to be your mother. She tried to keep you in her life," Nan added.

"And we didn't know how bad it was for you," Pop said, shaking his head. "We would have taken you sooner if we did. And I'm sorry for that. She kept you from us to hide what was really going on. But we should have known."

"Sometimes love makes excuses for people's behaviors. It can make you blind to the obvious," Nan added.

"But it is my fault that she died. If she hadn't been trying to be a better mom for me, she'd be alive." This was a fact. They must know it too. I ruined everyone's life. Her coming to me in my dreams was all the proof I needed.

"No, Tommy," Pop said, tapping my legs. "She was going to die from her addiction. You need to understand that. The accident was a freak event, but her love for you was what saved her from the drugs."

We sat in more silence while I took in their words. Maybe they were right. Maybe I needed to put this to rest. But still, it was hard not to see how it was not my fault. I had been a terrible son. I never got to talk to her again after the fight in the kitchen, and I wished then that she'd never come back.

"Can I have some of her ashes?"

"What do you plan on doing with them?" Nan asked.

"I want to hold a ceremony for her."

"Where?" Nan asked.

"Under the willow tree."

"That's not our property," Pop answered.

"Some of the branches are on our side."

"Okay," Nan quickly said. "I think that's a good idea. Now get some rest. How about you sleep with your door open and your light on?" She came over and kissed my forehead. "I love you."

"I love you, too," I answered.

Pop stayed with me until I drifted off to sleep. The next day, Nan handed me a nice ceramic jar that housed some of Mom's remains. I invited Roxy to join us. I changed into the only suit I had, which was getting too short in the arms and legs but would make do for an impromptu funeral. Nan, Pop, and Roxy all dressed up as well.

We huddled under the branches that fell on the property and watched as Pop took the shovel to dig the hole.

"Wait!" I said. "Maybe she wants to be free. What if she doesn't want to be in the ground?"

"Whatever you want to do, Tommy," Nan said.

"I want her to fly," I answered. "I don't want her to be trapped."

"Okay," Pop said, leaning the shovel against the garage.

We all stood around looking at each other, waiting for something.

"Normally, I like to say a few words before I put the mice to rest," Roxy finally spoke.

Nan had a very concerned look on her face but didn't say anything.

"She finds dead mice on glue traps and instead of throwing them in the trash, she buries them out here," I said.

"That makes more sense." Nan patted Roxy on the shoulders. "Because the way you said it made it sound as if you buried them alive."

"I would never," Roxy said, appearing somewhat insulted.

"Okay, let's do this." I stepped forward and cleared my throat. "Mom, I know you tried for me and I'm sorry that sometimes I would say I hate you because I love you." I paused and tried to come up with more to say, but what was there to say? I was still angry.

I passed Mom to Nan.

"You were my beautiful daughter. The moment I laid eyes on you, my whole life changed. My first child. A piece of me." Nan's eyes grew heavy with tears. "I will always love you like I did the day you were born. And you will always be that happy, crazy child that danced every chance you could get."

Nan passed Mom to Pop.

"Daddy's little girl." He stared at the ceramic container. "There are no words to say to make this okay. But I love you. I hope you know that. I hope you always knew that."

Pop handed Mom to Roxy.

"Tommy's mom, I didn't know you, but you made Tommy and he's my best friend. I promise to always take care of him. He's my family. So, wherever this wind takes you, know that I'll always be standing next to Tommy just like I am today."

Roxy handed Mom to me.

I opened the lid. Inside was Mom. Little, tiny pieces of what used to be a person. I waited until a gust of wind came along. I tossed the contents into the air, hoping they would catch the gust and they did. She flew away.

She never did return angry in my dreams. For the longest time, I never dreamt of her at all.

DUKE

I slept much of the day away because I was up all last night deciding how I feel about Kristy. I made a list like Mom suggested I do with colleges, which I still haven't done. I roll over and look at the clock, realizing that it's almost one pm. I grab the list and reread.

I'm embarrassed because my friends saw the kiss after I told them the truth. I guess that's my bad for saying anything to them in the first place. I'm mad because that's my girlfriend and I should have been the one kissing her. I'm infuriated that Kristy could actually kiss someone else and think it's not cheating because in my eyes it is. And I would never cheat on her. And I'm really pissed off that she ruined my big night.

All those things are still true; turns out sleep didn't magically erase my feelings. I have to tell her I can't do this anymore. I can't be some secret she keeps. Maybe she'll dump me and that leaves me feeling cold, but the other option is leaving me empty.

I text her and say we have to talk. I wait a few minutes, but she doesn't reply.

When I come out of my room, the house is fully alive; noise seems to be coming from every direction.

"You're up!" Mom says, coming through the living room. "Everyone, the guest of honor is awake."

From out back, I can hear people clapping.

"What's going on?" I say, suddenly feeling aware of my appearance.

"Go get ready, Duke. We're having a little party for you to celebrate the award you received last night."

"Really?" I ask, smiling.

"Of course," she answers, giving me a big hug. After she is down the hallway, I remember to yell out thank you.

I don't take my usual long while to get ready and Jayla already has been to my door warning me to hurry up. When I go out back, I find my dad and uncles are grilling. The picnic table is packed full of side dishes and someone has decorated the patio with ribbons and balloons of the school colors. My parents went all out. I spend all afternoon talking to everyone about football and what colleges are coming out to see me play. Last night's horribleness is starting to lift off me.

When I finally do check my phone, which I purposely left in my room, I have a ton of messages and missed calls. I quickly answer some back before my mom catches me. She has a few rules about the cell phone and one of them is to not be on it at family gatherings or I'll lose it for a day. I thought she was playing and found out the hard way one Christmas that she was not.

There is a party tonight at one of the cheerleader's houses whose parents are away and "of course, I have to be there," said Kristy and "of course we can talk there in private." I tell her I'll try depending on what time this party wraps up. I want to see her, and I don't want to see her. Maybe I'm just a chicken.

I text Tim back and ask to sleep at his house tonight because I'm planning on talking to Kristy and I don't want to have to be home at curfew. He answers back quick that I can and that his parents are out of town anyway. Time to party. He also reminds me that we don't have to pull a prank off to gain entrance into the party because it's just a small group of people.

Sophie started the grand tradition of the boys having to complete a task to get into her house a couple months ago. For the most part they are fun, like steal a construction sign or take selfies dressed up in suits. But I'm really glad that isn't happening tonight because I need to stay focused.

Out back I grab a chair next to Larry as he floats in and out of reality. Most of the family is starting to say goodbye, but in my family, it usually takes an hour from the moment someone says the first goodbye until you're actually sitting in a car.

"Little man," Larry says. "All this for you."

"Yeah," I answer. He's called me little man since I can remember and I'm so much taller than him.

"This family loves you."

"Yeah," I say. I watch my parents talking to my auntie and her new boyfriend. I can't believe they pulled this off without me even noticing.

"Love is good." He sips his beer. "Love like this can never hurt you. No matter where you go in life, you'll always have this. Remember that."

"I will."

"This life is taking you places."

"You think?" I ask. Sometimes I use Larry like a fortune teller. He's surprisingly accurate. He always knows when my parents will be really upset at something that I think is not a big deal. Like the time I left my dad with no gas. Larry told me to leave ten dollars by his keys to make him think I was responsible. He did notice and asked me if I could fill the tank next time. Lecture avoided. It's nice to have a warning system.

"Yes. Don't even second guess it. Just run toward it like you're waiting for a football to float into your hands." He gestures with hands out to the great beyond.

"Okay, Larry, I will."

"Whatever opportunities life gives you, you say yes."

"Okay."

"Don't be scared to fly because we all got you. Just like you all got me."

After the last guest leaves, I ask my parents if I can sleep over at Tim's house after I clean up, which they agree to. Jayla already has her best friend over for a sleepover, so they help me clean until Tim's car pulls up.

"Duke," Jayla starts in. "Last night wasn't cool. Don't pay her no mind tonight."

"Thanks."

"I mean it, Duke. I may be younger than you, but right now I'm giving you the advice you'd give to me. Think about." She turns back to the sink and rinses the last dish.

I know she's right. If this were her, I would have already been in the guy's face.

Tim drives to the party and I haven't come up with a good plan to deal with Kristy. I should stay mad. I should ignore her. But the truth is I want to see her. I hate the way I feel. I shouldn't be going to this stupid party, but it's too late because we are here.

Kristy is sitting at the kitchen table when we walk in, beer in her hand.

"There he is," she announces to the room. "That's my boyfriend."

I freeze. The room is too small. There's not enough air.

"Come here, Duke." She stands and walks toward me. "It's just our closest friends. No one will tell. Right, guys? You won't tell my dad and you won't tell anyone at school?"

"We won't tell a soul," one of the cheerleader's pipes in.

She hugs me tight. "I'm so sorry about last night. I want to make it up to you." She places her hands on my cheeks and pulls my mouth towards hers. "You going to kiss me or what?"

I give her a small kiss, testing the waters in case she slaps me, but she doesn't. She kisses me back.

"We still have to talk," I whisper.

"We will. In a little bit, I promise." She grabs my hand and leads me to the table.

"Okay, let the games begin," Tim announces. All night we sit around the table playing king's cup. It feels wrong that my parents threw me a party today and here I am drinking.

Kristy makes a rule when she draws an eight and makes me drink every time she drinks. At some point during the game, she decided that my lap would be her new seat.

This feeling of us actually being a couple in front of people is the most freeing experience. But even so, I can't seem to touch her with ease in front of watchful eyes.

We play until Tim draws the last king and has to drink the pitcher of beer in the middle of the table.

"Done!" He slams down the container and kisses Sophie. It's going to be that kind of night. The kind of night that Tim will be puking in the toilet.

"Come with me," Kristy says and leads me upstairs to the guest bedroom and closes the door.

"Are you still mad about last night?" she asks.

"I'm not happy," I say and sit on the bed.

She leans against the closed bedroom door. "I'm really sorry about what happened."

"I need the Wyatt thing to end," I say and look away. I feel weak for needing it to stop, but strong for saying it.

"He's our cover. Without him, it's back me not being able to talk on the phone or drive you home from practice."

"I'm fine with that. I'm not fine with seeing you kiss someone else."

"It's not cheating, Duke. I'm doing it for us."

"I don't want an 'us' if it means Wyatt is involved. I can't handle it." My fist clenches as the thought of them kissing flashes in my mind.

She looks at me and begins to say something but changes her mind.

"Kristy, I'm sorry, but I can't do it."

"If that's what you need, I'll take care of it. I don't want to make you mad."

"Thank you." I look at her and her face softens.

"Are you happy now?"

"A little," I answer.

She comes toward me and takes her shirt off.

"How about now? Are you happy now?" she says, running her hands on my face.

"Kristy, I don't need you to take your clothes off to make me happy."

"I'm not taking them off for that reason."

"Then what reason are you taking them off for?"

"Because I'm in love with you and I'm ready." She kisses me.

My hands shake in excitement as I touch her smooth skin. "I love you, too. You know that, right?"

"I know that, Duke."

"Like really love you, though, like can't ever stop thinking about you. Even if I'm mad at you."

"I do. I know you love me and you're never going to hurt me."

"Never. It's me and you." We kiss that long kiss that feels like you're actually talking to the person. Like you're really opening your heart and pouring it all out.

"Are you ready, Duke?"

"Yes. I'm ready."

She leans over and turns out the light.

THE ORIGINAL WRECK: SURRENDER

TOMMY: AGE 13

I knew exactly what I was getting Roxy for Christmas, though it was only Thanksgiving and I'd have to wait an entire month to hand her the wrapped box under my bed. To say that Nan didn't understand would be an understatement, I think she went along knowing she had time to take me to get another gift. But what I got Roxy was perfect.

Thanksgiving dinner had always been celebrated at Nan and Pop's house, though I did miss on more than one occasion when Mom would forget that the holiday was even occurring. I didn't like it much, but mostly because of my cousins. They come over with their inside jokes which I always thought were about me. They stuck together and even if they hated each other at times, they bonded together to keep people like me on the outside.

When they came over to the house, they would head to the basement and straight for the television. Of course, they had manners, they would make a beeline after they said hello to the grandparents, but they wouldn't even wave at me. It was as if I was infected with a disease they could catch just by looking at me. If I wandered down to see what they were up to, they would act like I wasn't there. Of course, I didn't say much to them while observing their sibling behaviors. Their inclusiveness somehow always left me wanting. My grandparents tried fixing the problem, but you can't force people to like each other. I think they felt bad for me, like I was missing out on something. But I knew I wasn't.

This year I decided not to follow them down. Instead, I went outside to be with Roxy, who waited patiently for me by the graveyard of last year's vegetable garden. The best thing about best friends is their willingness to keep you company while your family shunned you. And being that Roxy's family wouldn't even know where she was, we were the perfect fit.

Roxy had spent the last few weeks collecting discarded whole pumpkins from our neighbors who bored with Halloween decorations fast and trashed them. She had a nice collection of six round, perfectly orange pumpkins ready for carving, just the thing to pass time while Thanksgiving dinner cooked. She even embezzled the perfect carving knives in the sweatshirt she stood holding.

"I have the directions in my pocket," she said, big, toothy grin on her face. What she wanted was to win the town carving competition next year. The grand prize was five hundred dollars, and she wanted to buy a guitar so we could officially start our band. We had each gotten very good at playing, thanks to all the lessons and YouTube. This year she took seventh place, which in my opinion, was pretty good since there were over a hundred contestants. She only allowed herself to smile for three seconds before she already started dreaming of what to do for next year. On the way to school the following Monday morning, she already had her plan formed. And the design, if she could pull it off, would be spectacular, and a sure victory.

She had found an anglerfish design she fell in love with and would allow her to enter the spooky category—her favorite. Anglerfish are proof that aliens do exist, maybe not in the form people think but rather in the depths of the ocean. I tried to get her to find a less complicated carving idea, but she was hell bent and found six pumpkins to start practicing on. When the weather warmed, she planned to move on to watermelons. There was no talking her out of it.

"It's for the PETA's, Tommy," she said. "We are good, but imagine what we'll be like with two guitars. This is my shot to not only get a guitar but other equipment too. Five hundred bucks can go a long way."

I had to agree with her because there was no way her parents were getting her a guitar. So many birthdays and Christmases had past, each with disappointment. Her mother told her respectfully that she couldn't stand listening to her practice. Nan and Pop wouldn't mind if she stored her guitar at our house and only practiced there. This really was her only opportunity until we could get part-time jobs.

We walked quietly around Pop's shed to the back wall hidden from any parental eyes. The fall air was crisp with winter chill nipping at our ankles. The brown, crunchy leaves that covered the ground made a nice blanket for us to place the pumpkins to carve on.

I was in charge of gutting the pumpkins so she could focus solely on the design element. We worked in quiet with just the noise of the knives slicing into the pumpkin's flesh sitting between us. Roxy's first few attempts at getting the teeth just right were terrible, though better than anything that I could have done. I never had the steady hand in carving, even the lids I was carving out were not close to a circle. But by the fifth pumpkin she found her way.

"Tommy, look!" She spun the pumpkin to face me. "I did it."

"Holy crap, that actually looks good," I said, looking behind her at the four discarded attempts that rested against the shed.

"I know. I'm going to win." She spun the pumpkin around and went back to work.

I continued to shovel the guts out and toss them in the dead leaves next to me when I heard her laughing. "What's so funny?" I asked.

When she didn't answer, I finally looked over and saw bright red blood dripping down her hand and onto the ground. She stood and grabbed her hand, squeezing it tight.

"It's okay," I lied. "Let's just go to my house and get a Band-Aid." I knew we would be in trouble if we got caught. Her more than me. I led her to the front door so we could sneak to the upstairs bathroom. I shut us into the bathroom and turned the sink on, making Roxy put her hand under the faucet. Blood was gushing out of the wound that was on her left hand by her thumb. A huge, gaping incision that I had no clue how to fix. Roxy was white as a ghost.

"I think I need to get someone to help us," I said, panic crawling up my throat.

"No! I don't want to get in trouble," she cried.

"I'll tell them it was my idea," I pleaded with her. And then she passed out.

I ran downstairs in a frenzy and all the adults came running back with me. She was coming to on the floor when Pop ran next door to tell her family. I watched from the window as they loaded her in the car, her hand wrapped in Nan's fancy white hand towel, now a dark pink. I could hear my cousins whispering about me from the living room they were in.

I didn't manage to tell Roxy's parents that it was my idea.

"Let's go clean up," Pop said coming and standing next to me. We watched as the taillights blinked out as they turned the corner. "That wasn't one of the best ideas you two had." I could hear the disappointment in his voice as I followed out back.

He handed me a bag and instructed me to trash all evidence while he took care of the knives.

"I know this wasn't your idea, Tommy, so why did you lie?" He stopped moving to study my face.

I paused picking up the remnants and looked up. "How do you know? I could have thought of this," I mouthed back. I never gave any lip to him, but to insinuate that I couldn't come up with this plan was somewhat insulting.

"One reason would be that you don't like carving pumpkins enough to do it multiple times," he said as he pointed to the trash bag that housed all the pumpkins. "Another would be that these aren't our knives." He waved the knives in the air. "And finally, and most important, is that all Roxy has been talking about is winning the carving competition next year." He looked hard at me.

"Fine. It wasn't my idea." I hung my head in defeat. "Don't tell Roxy's parents that."

"It's fine to cover for friends, but when it's serious like this, you have to tell the truth." He put his hand on my shoulder.

"She'll get in trouble."

"As she should. And you're in trouble too."

"I mean like real trouble, Pop."

Lately it seemed like all Roxy could do was get in trouble. There had been so many evenings that we have snuck out to the willow tree to sit while she cried about being yelled at for things that weren't in her control. Like every time her dad came home and found her mother had gone out with her friends without leaving him dinner. Somehow Roxy was to blame.

"What do you mean, Tommy? Does someone hurt Roxy?" I could tell my answer really mattered to him. Like maybe he would do or say something to Roxy's family. I knew right then that Roxy would be pissed at me for life.

"No, they don't hurt her. But they will be really tough on her. Pop, please just let me take the blame," I begged.

We stood silent behind the shed for a long time. I could smell all the neighbor's turkey dinners cooking away. This was not how this day was supposed to go. And now I didn't know what Pop would do with the information I gave him. I should have fought harder to take the blame. I should have insisted that it was my idea.

He gave me no indication of what his thoughts were. Instead, he told me to go wash up for dinner and that I was grounded.

Later that night when I said goodnight to Nan, she told me that Roxy would have to have surgery on her hand because she cut through some important things, but for now she was home with several stiches.

Under my bed sat the wrapped shirt I had made. Two guitar silhouettes with The PETA's in black, bold lettering layered over them. I never did get to give it to her. Sometime after I watched Pop walk the knives back to her house, Roxy must have made up her mind that I was a bad friend because she never spoke to me again.

DUKE

Sometimes I randomly feel guilty for growing up. It's just this thing that happens to my parents' faces when my sister and I have plans on a Saturday night. It goes like this:

"Hey, Duke, college football tonight," Dad says. He's always extremely enthusiastic, big hand gestures, wide smile.

"I can't tonight, Dad, I told the squad I'd watch it with them over at Tim's house."

The smile fades away, the eyes cast down to the floor, the lips curl up like he ate something that didn't agree with him. All this takes only a few seconds and then it's back to being enthusiastic and saying, way too loud, "Another time then." It was simpler back in middle school when it was expected for you to be the built-in friends your parents thought of you as, companions by default.

"Duke," Mom hollers from the kitchen. "Come here."

I come in and find her making herself a cup of tea. She steeps the bag in a steaming hot cup of water.

"I was thinking we should get something for the kid who is tutoring you. What's his name again?" She steps on the bottom of the trash can and the lid flies open.

"His name is Tommy."

"What do you think I should get him? I'm doing some sofa shopping tonight."

"I don't know." I lean against the refrigerator.

"What do you mean you don't know? You've been with him for a while now. What does he like?"

"He's kind of really quiet and doesn't talk about personal stuff, Mom."

"That's not helpful at all."

"Sorry to disappoint, but really he doesn't talk to anyone at school, so it's not like I can ask around. I know that's going to be your next question."

"You know me so well." She laughs at herself. "Just give me something to go on. Something little."

"He loves math. I have to go, Mom. I'll be home by curfew."

"No talking to the ladies." She laughs as I leave the kitchen. At least I know Jayla hasn't told her about Kristy yet. That's pretty cool of her to keep it to herself. Usually that hot head would tell the whole family any gossip about me.

The late October air already has a little winter chill in it. I run the few blocks to Tim's house, partly out of the cold and partly for the exercise. I need to be faster than I was the day before. "Be a better version than the yesterday's version of yourself," that's what Coach is always yelling at us. Push harder. Dig deeper.

"Duke," a few of my teammates call out to me in a low, steady cheer. It's a cheer I'm used to after a touchdown. A hard D followed by a long U and a short K. I love it.

They shift their bodies on the sofa and make room for me to sit.

"Where have you been? You missed a sick return kick," Tim says as he hands me a soda. "Staring at yourself in the mirror again?"

"You know it. How could anyone not stop and admire?" I say, touching my cheeks.

"I know a certain cheerleader who will be taking a long look tonight," Smookler says. "Party at Sophie's house."

"Oh yeah?" I feign interest even though I'm excited. Kristy hasn't been able to talk to me just like she said she wouldn't be able to once she broke up with Wyatt. And I miss her.

The game is over around eight and the talk about who is going to get with who is already starting up when Tim's phone dings with a text.

"Gentleman, gentleman," Tim speaks over us. "Entrance for tonight's party is Tom Moffe's truck parked out front of Sophie's house. Requested by and credit given to Kristy."

Every inch of my body tightens. What is Kristy thinking? Maybe Tim read that wrong. She knows Tommy is my tutor. Is she trying to embarrass me? Or have Tommy hate me so he won't tutor me anymore? Does she think this is funny?

I don't get it. I don't get her. I check my phone to see if she texted me. Nothing.

"Who the hell is Tom Moffe?" someone yells out.

"Isn't that the weird kid that tutors you, Duke?" Tim asks.

"You've got all the brains you need for the field," Smookler says, throwing an awkward high-five up.

My cheeks are burning red. I want to tell him I'm not dumb, but instead say that Coach wanted me to get into a good college.

Tim's phone dings with another text.

"And in case we were trying to cheat, they want to be clear that Tom is not invited to the party nor can he drive the truck there himself."

"We have to steal the truck?" I ask. I feel the sudden need to vomit. How can she sleep with me and say she loves me and then do this?

"Where does this nerdtard live?" Tim ignores my question.

"We can't steal his truck, guys. We could get arrested," I remind them.

"If we get caught all you have to do is threaten him a bit. He won't press charges. Come on, Duke, I'm so close to closing the deal with Sophie. Don't ruin this for me." Tim slaps my shoulder. I want to tell him that maybe he could actually have a relationship with Sophie if he stops drinking to the point of throwing up, but decide now is not the time.

"Duke, let's go!" Smookler is yelling like we are on the field and this is the last play of the game.

I have zero time to think before someone is yelling about how Duke doesn't want to hurt his boyfriend's feelings. So mature. Tim is practically pleading with me and I should care since he is the reason I may be getting a scholarship, but grand theft auto so he can get some ass doesn't seem like a favor you ask your best friend.

"Guys, Coach would freak out. Text her back and ask for something else."

"Pussy," someone yells.

"Come on, Duke. Don't be a pussy. Let's just go see the truck." Tim grabs his keys and starts up the basement stairs.

"Fine." I follow behind like the baby bitch that I am.

Smookler yells that he found the address as we leave Tim's house. I think of ways I could stall and come up with nothing. The whole drive over, I plead with God that Tommy will be out. When Tim pulls onto Tommy's street, he kills his headlights and parks a few houses away.

"This is such a stupid idea," I mumble.

We have a hurried, offensive meeting by the cars and decide that Smookler and I will go to investigate the truck while the others are on lookout. If anyone spots trouble, they will let out a loud whistle. No one appreciates when I complain about how obvious that is.

Down the road, Smookler and I move like two burglars in the night. I'm not going to lie, it is kind of fun, but when I see the truck in the driveway, I want to sprint back to my house.

Smookler has balls of steel though. He moves right up to the driver's side door and opens it.

"This asshole left the keys in the ignition," he whispers. "Get in and put the truck in neutral and I'll push you into the road."

"No way. You do it." I move to the front of the truck before he can argue, the whole time silently apologizing to Tommy. Smookler gives the thumps-up and I push the truck like it's a tackle dummy on the football field. The truck eases into the street where Smookler turns the key and the engine roars to life.

I'm running back down the street to Tim's car as if there are bullets chasing me. The cold air nips at my face, creating tears in my eyes. But if I'm honest, the tears are real. I'm the biggest dick I know. That kid has been nothing but nice to me.

Smookler parks the truck in Sophie's driveway and they all head in. I linger back and look to see if he left the keys in the ignition too, but he didn't.

I want to throw up. I want to call Tommy. I want to go home.

"I can't believe you pulled it off," Kristy says, coming out to the driveway. "I knew you wanted to see me really bad, but this, Duke, this is love."

"Why would you ask me to do this? What is wrong with you?" I pace around the truck. "He's a good person."

"Calm down, Duke. We'll take the truck back in a little bit."

"Calm down? You want me to calm down? I just stole a car. For what? To get into a party so I can see you?"

"That kid isn't even going to notice. Come inside and stop freaking out. Don't you want to spend time with me? I've missed you." She walks toward me.

"Get away from me."

"What? Why are you so mad?"

"Because you say you love me and then you make me do something horrible to a friend of mine."

"He's not your friend, Duke, he's your tutor."

"That's where you're wrong. He's both."

"Just come inside." She reaches for my hand, but I swat it away. "Duke, quit playing games."

"I'm not playing games. You are."

"You need to come inside with me."

"No. I don't need to do anything with you. We are done." The words escape my mouth before I can really think about what I'm saying.

"You're breaking up with me over a stupid prank?"

"I don't know what I'm doing and it's not stupid. I trusted you."

"Oh yeah, keep telling yourself that. You fuck me and then you dump me. Some good guy you are."

"Some good girlfriend you are."

"You promised you wouldn't hurt me," she says, crying.

"You're the one that did this, not me."

"You promised."

"I have to get out of here. Away from you. I need to be alone right now." I turn and walk away.

"Duke, get back here," she hollers.

I don't bother turning around. I can't stop shaking. The anger is a drug that has seized my body.

THE ORIGINAL WRECK: AFTERSHOCK

TOMMY: AGE 13

Winter dragged on with an endless pit of darkness that absorbed every fiber of my body. At some point, I unwrapped the shirt only to wrap it again, vowing to win her back as a friend. It felt like I lost a vital organ and was suffering from a slow and very painful death. I rode the bus in silence as the other kids laughed all around me. Her empty seat carved a hole in my chest, leaving only a sterile heart in which blood and muscle performed its mandatory duty of beating.

Roxy hadn't taken the bus since the incident. In school, I would only see glimpses of her walking the halls or in the cafeteria. Her hand was in a cast that was stuffed in a sling. So many names graffitied the plaster, all but one it seemed. I tried to get close to her any way I could. I threw out my entire lunch, hoping to catch her at the trash can. I went hungry for the rest of the day, left only with the knowledge that she turned slowly and intentionally away from me.

It seemed as if she became a ghost overnight. A memory from long ago that used to be but ceased to exist. In the newfound time I had in her absence, I would create mock scenarios of how to accidentally run into her and beg for her to be friends again.

But when I had my chance I failed. In the beginning, I would go to the library and sit at our favorite table, the one by the huge window that looked out into the park. Roxy loved this seat the best because there was also a view of the front door, which came in handy while I waited for her. On more than one occasion, she opened the library door and saw me sitting there only to turn around and leave. It wasn't until I realized I could hide among the rows of books and go unnoticed, allowing her time to get into the building, that I was successful.

I waited for her to get deep into the library before I let my breath out. The woman in the aisle with me grew impatient with my blocking the author she was looking to find. I moved up the row, running my hand down the spines of the books. Roxy and I knew this place inside and out. We sat in this very section for hours playing a game she made up. We would each open a book and only read the third paragraph down on page 367 to see what kind of new stories we could create out of the material. Sometimes the books didn't have that page and we would subtract by fifty until we had a page to read from. Our new stories mostly never made sense, which made us laugh even harder. Roxy always came up with the best games.

I knew whatever I was going to say I needed to say it fast before she stormed off. I debated for several minutes and landed on starting the conversation out with an apology. I wasn't entirely sure what I was apologizing for, but it needed to work. By the time I got close enough to her, I changed my mind again. I would say I missed her.

My mind circulated so heavily between "I'm sorry" and "I miss you" that I didn't even notice her looking at me. She dropped the book she was holding and walked out of the library. *I miss you. I'm sorry.* Just thoughts trapped in my head.

I promised myself I had time to come up with a better plan and when that time came, I wouldn't screw it up.

So, when I woke one Saturday morning in early January to find a For Sale sign on the front of her lawn, I could do only one thing: panic. I didn't even bother to change out of my pajamas before I tore downstairs and out the front door.

I stood next to the red-and-white sign looking for answers, but the sign revealed nothing. I ran to the back door and knocked without once thinking about what I would say.

When her father answered, I was past the point of reasonable, crying. "Is Roxy home?" I asked between sobs.

"No, she's not," he said from behind the glass door. He looked me up and down. I knew I looked a mess. Besides the tears that flowed with great ease down my face, there was also my unbrushed hair that I could tell was sticking up, along with my way-too-small blue PETA t-shirt Roxy got me, and just socks because there was no time to stop for shoes.

"What's going on here? Where are you guys going? Why are you moving? Why does she hate me?" My body shook in the wake of the sudden grief. "She's leaving me without a goodbye."

"Okay, okay," he said and opened the door enough to reach his arm out to touch my shoulder. "You need to calm down. Look, Tommy, sometimes in life, friendships don't make it and it is sad, but it happens all the time."

"Not to Roxy and me it doesn't happen."

"Roxy has moved on for her own personal reasons and maybe one day she'll explain that to you. Who knows? The only advice I can give you is that you've got to let it go and move on."

"I don't want to. Not without talking to her first."

"She decided that she doesn't want to talk to you, so you have to respect her. Besides, we are moving today."

"Today?"

"Roxy's grandmother is sick, and we have to move in and take care of her. I'm sorry, kiddo. Best of luck to you." He shut the glass door and then the big door and just like that, it was over. I knew he would never miss me, but the harsh simplicity of it all made me shiver.

I walked back to my house, debating if I should go back over and open their door, search every room in the house until I found her and demand that she speak to me. But my feet dragged me away from my heart, knowing I wouldn't make it past her dad.

I sat on the front porch the rest of the day, watching the moving trucks come and pack everything up. Watched as they took her bedroom furniture out the front door and deep into the belly of the truck. Watched as they carried boxes labeled "Roxy's bedroom" one by one from the house and packed snugged, heading to a destination far from me. I wondered if all the things we made together were in those boxes. Like the amazing popsicle fortress we erected that came not only with a tower but also a horse stable per Roxy's request, lovingly called Roxy's Fortress of Fun.

As I watched them systemically take everything away from me, I hoped against all hope that Roxy would appear, but she never did.

"Tommy, it's dark out here and cold," Pop said, coming out onto the porch. "Why don't you come in and warm up? Maybe she'll be back tomorrow."

"What did you say to them when you took the knives back at Thanksgiving?" I asked.

My body was shivering even though I had warm clothes on and a winter coat. At some point, the rain had started, and the damp air left my clothes feeling waterlogged.

"I told them that the knives belonged to them." Pop grabbed a seat on the porch swing next to me. "Why?"

"Because that's when she decided to hate me, and I don't understand why. Maybe because I didn't cover for her. I just want to know."

"We don't always get to know why things happen, Tommy."

"I know that, Pop. I understand that, but this can't happen with Roxy. She's my best friend. We don't just move and not say goodbye."

"I'm so sad for you, Tommy, I really am. This breaks my heart to watch you. I know you love her like a sister. And I'm so sorry you have to feel this pain. I wish I could tell you why Roxy is behaving like this, but I can't."

"Did her parents say anything when you gave the knives back? Maybe they hinted that Roxy was mad at me? Maybe they were mad at me and thought I was a bad person?"

"No, Tommy, they didn't say a word."

"I just want to understand so bad." My chest felt like there was an octopus squeezing with all of its tentacles, cutting off circulation to the rest of my body. The pain was overwhelming. I didn't know I was gasping for air until Pop started patting my back and instructing me to breathe slowly.

"One minute at a time, Tommy. That's all you have to focus on. Deep breaths, now."

We sat swinging for a while more before Pop made me go in. I ate half a grilled cheese sandwich Nan made and went to bed. I woke early and resumed watch on the porch, but she never did come back.

The worst part of losing a friend is the wanting. The wanting to tell them when something funny happens, or if you want to ride bikes, or if you want to go to the movies. I spent all my time wanting.

I spent the whole rest of the year wandering around in silence, wishing I could just see her. Wishing we could camp out in the backyard as she promised and build us the best tree fort ever. My birthday came and went and so did hers. I imagined all the fun stories she would have told me from her trip to the shore, not to mention the endless days we would swim in the pool.

But as it was, I spent most of the summer under our willow tree reading books I checked out from her most favorite place in the world, the library. And when I was good and hollow from the sadness, it was time for school to start again. A big year, my grandparents said, 9th grade was a year of opportunity.

Of course, I knew what they meant. They wanted me to meet new friends and move on from Roxy, but I would never let that happen. I would never allow someone to take her place or have the opportunity to crush me.

I decided friendship equaled needing and besides my grandparents, I needed no one. And the reality was that no one needed me.

DUKE

I circle the block, trying to decide if I should go back to the party and take the keys from Smookler. I feel like I'm losing my mind. I don't think this is what love should feel like. It shouldn't feel like I'm losing everything to make someone happy. I know that much.

Kristy is blowing up my phone. She hates me and never wants to see me again. I pause and lean against the stop sign. My mind races all around, but the loop it's stuck on is the night I slept with Kristy. The way our bodies seemed like one as we slept through the night. I woke up several times that night and laid in the darkness feeling whole. But tonight, she was someone else, practically laughing at my feelings, as if what I was saying didn't matter to her. And now somewhere out there, Tommy has no clue his truck is gone. I did this. I took the only thing that I've seen make him happy.

There is no easy answer, but I land on go back to the party and get the truck, but then start walking in the direction of home. "I didn't mean to do this," I say out loud. I'm a coward.

I cross the street and start walking through town. I wish I could call someone. No, I wish I could call Tommy and apologize. I give up on walking and take a seat on the bench by the bus stop, hoping sitting will help stop my racing heart.

Kristy's texts have stopped coming through. It's a relief in some sense, but I'm fighting the urge to text her back and start this fight all over again. She doesn't deserve to have the last word.

"Hey, perv." Charlie's voice floats over to me.

I spin around and see her walking out of the coffeehouse. She looks different with her hair in a ponytail.

"You look like shit. Are you okay?" she asks, coming toward me.

"I'm fine," I answer way too short.

"Yeah, totally looks like you are. Why are you sweating so much?"

"I'm not." I wipe my forehead.

"Well, it's none of my business." She grabs a seat next to me.

"I'm not in the mood to talk," I say, shifting in my seat. She smells of coffee and cake.

"Great. I'm not trying to talk to you, but we are in fact waiting for the bus in the designated waiting area."

"You're taking the bus? To where?" I say, looking around.

"Home. I just got done with work."

"I've never been on the bus before," I say mostly to myself.

"You have lived a sheltered life, my friend."

We drift into silence for some time before my phone begins to blow up with texts. Tim wants to know where I am because Kristy is crying and ruining his chances with Sophie. Nothing about the fact that we need to get Tommy's truck back.

"Are you getting on the bus and going somewhere?" she finally asks.

"No. Just resting."

"Make sense. Here's an idea though, you can tell me what's wrong."

"What makes you think something is wrong?"

"All of this. It's nine o'clock on a Saturday night and you're sitting at a bus stop with no plans to actually get on the bus. That all sounds like something is wrong."

"I did something bad." I spill the whole story out in fast sentences so I'm left winded. I look over to her and see the disgust on her face. I've never seen her mad. Frustrated, yes. But this look on her face right now is new to me.

"I can't believe you, Duke. Why would you do that?"

"I don't know. It happened so fast and who would have thought the keys were in the truck? I'm sorry." I bow my head in shame. I'm a terrible person. I can feel that all the way to my core.

"Get up." She stands and starts walking away.

"Where are you going?" I follow her.

"To get Tom's truck back."

"You're going in the wrong direction," I yell after her.

"Well, lead the way then." She storms past me, so I have to jog to get ahead of her to get us going in the right direction.

We walk back to the party with no plan on how we are going to pull this off. Or maybe she has a plan in her head, but she is certainly not sharing it with me.

When we get a few houses away, I start to panic. What if they won't give the keys back? What if the football team hates me? What if Kristy starts her crap again?

I'm so mad at all of them. But I care what they think. I hate that I care. I hate it.

"Stay here," Charlie says.

"Don't you need me to go in?"

"Why would I need you to walk into a party? You're just going to slow me down."

She walks into the house like she was invited. I'm left on the sidewalk like a reject. A few minutes later, she comes running out of the house.

"Let's go," she yells and throws the keys at me. "Hurry up."

I run after her to the truck, but I'm not fast enough. Kristy is lightning quick running from the front door.

"I see you already have another girlfriend ready to do your dirty work." She's screaming. "You're a real class act, Duke. Scumbag." She chucks her empty beer can at me and it hits my chest. I shut and lock the driver's door.

"Shit. Shit. Shit." I speak fast. "I forgot this is a stick."

"Push the clutch in and turn the key to start the car," Charlie is hollering at me. I stall several times before completing the task of just turning the car on. Kristy has started banging on the truck when Charlie hops out.

"He's just going to use you. He'll sleep with you and then dump you." Kristy is crying. "He did it to me. You won't be different. I thought he loved me."

"I'm not trying to have sex with Duke. Tom is my friend and I want his truck returned to him. That's all. Go inside and we'll never speak of this again. You and Duke can work out your stuff tomorrow."

"He won't talk to me." Kristy yells right at me. "You just get mad and walk away? You think that's okay? I want him to talk to me."

"He will tomorrow. I promise. It's probably better that you guys don't talk now anyway. You're both upset. Just go inside and he'll talk to you tomorrow. Isn't that right, Duke?" Charlie is pleading with me.

"Yes. I promise," I say. I can hardly look at Kristy, but I do long enough so she believes me.

"Okay, I'll go inside." She stumbles and catches herself on the truck.

Charlie walks her back to the house and returns to the truck. "Let's go," she says, her words full of fury.

We barely manage to find reverse and stall several more times driving down the road. Thankfully Tommy lives close and no major roads are required to get this truck back to its rightful home.

"We pushed it out of the driveway," I say as we get closer to his house.

"Well, we can't push it back in," she says, looking out her window. "Just kill the headlights and we'll have to be very fast getting out of the truck."

"Something smells bad. Like it's burning," I say.

"You probably messed something up."

"Fuck." I kill the headlights and pull into his driveway. We both get out fast, trying to gently shut the doors. We make it a block away before she speaks again.

"What you did tonight, Duke, is gross."

"I know."

"I'm so disappointed in you as a person. I thought you were better than this."

"I am." Her words cut me in ways I wasn't prepared for.

"I know we're not friends, but I always thought you were cool. You could walk around school like some hot shot with a big head, but you never do that. You talk to anyone as if everyone is equal and there is no social pyramid with you at the top. So why now? Why treat Tommy like shit?"

"Sometimes it feels like I'm losing control. It feels like everything is connected and if I don't do what everyone expects me to do, then I'm going to lose it all. I'm lucky to have what I have and maybe one day the wind is going to change directions and I'll be left with nothing."

"Duke, you're not lucky. You're talented because you worked for it. There's a difference. And nothing in this world should change you from being a nice person. Not football and not Kristy," she says, her voice still sounding angry.

"I know."

We continue down the road, just the sound of our footsteps between us.

"What happens if Tom finds out it was you? Are you going to tell him?"

"I don't know," I answer. Telling Tommy just means he'll hate me sooner rather than later.

"You really need to think about things," she says as we walk back to the bus stop. "You don't have to wait."

"When's the next bus coming?"

"Thirty minutes."

"I'm not letting you sit out here alone."

"It's fine really. I do it all the time."

"Well, I'm staying. You don't have to talk to me."

"And I won't," she answers.

"And just so you know, back there when we were walking, you said that we aren't friends, and I think that we are," I say. She stares straight ahead never looking over at me.

We sit in silence until the bus comes. She says goodbye, but nothing more. I sit alone for another twenty minutes before deciding to walk home.

My house is dark and quiet when I come in. My parents' television is on in their bedroom. They always try to wait up for me to check in. I peek my head in the door and see my dad drifting in and out of sleep. He would be so disappointed in me.

"You are home," he says.

"Safe and sound. Go back to sleep." I slip out of the door and go to my room. I pull down my old lunch box I used to carry around in elementary school. The faded players of the Philadelphia Eagles have kept my money safe for years. I count the bills even though I know there is four hundred and fifty-six dollars. I'll just give this to Tommy and say it's for the tutoring in case he needs it to fix his truck.

THE SECONDARY WRECK: LIFE AFTER DEATH

TOMMY: AGE 17

I wake to another dream of Mom, making it the fourth dream of her in two weeks. I haven't had a dream of her in so many years, and what's even more disturbing about these dreams is the fact that I haven't aged one bit. It is like we are frozen in time forever. I am forever twelve and she is forever thirty-four. She's beautiful and full of life, not pale and skinny, but healthy and happy. She doesn't say much, but there is a way about her that makes me feel like she is proud of me.

Perhaps she's coming to me now since I finished applying to colleges. My list is long, but the most important application is Princeton University. My belly turns with dread, knowing it's all about the waiting game to hear back.

When I come downstairs, Nan already has the grocery list made and money waiting for me on the counter next to my anxiety pill bottle. Four years in the making and I've never missed a day of taking it, yet she always feels the need to put it out when she's not around in the morning.

I take the last bit of coffee and fill a thermos before heading out the door. My truck is not parked in its usual spot. It's too far over to the right and a little cock-eyed. I must have been tired when I got back from the library yesterday.

The first thing I notice about the truck is that it is very hard to change gears, but I run to the food store anyway. Grocery shopping is my tradeoff for having the truck, Pop said, when he handed me the keys. He told me how much Nan hated it lately and he never enjoyed it either.

But I do enjoy it. I find it fascinating what people put in their carts. I play a game every week called, *What are you buying and why?* The most obvious contestants can be found in the specialty aisles, like gluten-free or organic. But I like to find the ones who seem to be hunting down something very special, like maybe a husband in a panic trying to buy flowers and balloons for his wife. I always want to stop them and ask, "But does she really want this? Maybe there's a better gift that says, 'I didn't forget you' and that gift is not at the grocery store."

One morning I followed an elderly lady around who was buying things she was reading off a recipe card. She eventually realized I was following her, so I had to confess that my curiosity got the best of me. She told me she was making her best friend's favorite casserole in honor of their fifty years of friendship.

But today I shop fast, hoping to catch Pop before he goes out to play cards with his friends. When I pull into the driveway, he is already walking to his car.

"Hey, Pop," I say, rolling down my window. "Do you have a minute?"

He takes the truck around the block and diagnoses it with a bad clutch.

"Have you been grinding the gears?" he asks.

"No."

"Maybe last night since you must have forgotten how to drive. I noticed this morning that your truck was parked in the middle of the driveway, so I moved it."

"I didn't park in the middle of the driveway."

"I'm telling you, you did. I moved it myself." He pulls back into our driveway.

"No way."

"Okay, let's go look at the video. If I'm right, you give me a hundred dollars," he says and smiles.

"Double or nothing." I hold out my hand and we shake.

It takes a minute to get the video to back up to yesterday, but that's when I see it.

"Go forward," I say.

He clicks the time forward. There on the screen two people are running up to my truck and hopping in. One pushes the truck into the street and then turns the engine on while the other runs away.

"Who is this, Tommy?"

"I don't know. Can you go forward to when they return it?"

He clicks the time forward to when the truck comes back into the driveway and two people get out.

"They stole your truck!" Pop says. "Do you know them?"

"No," I answer. But I do know them. Duke is in both screen shots and Charlie is in the last one.

"Well, we have to call the police," Pop says, taking a long sigh.

"No, we don't. The police won't be able to do anything, and I left the keys in the truck."

"What have I told you about that?"

"I know, Pop. I'm sorry."

"I'm calling the police." He walks to the phone.

"Don't. I lied. I do know them. Let me get to the bottom of this."

"I hope these aren't new friends of yours," Pop says, walking to the door to leave. "It's going to cost a couple hundred bucks to fix it, so you better get the money from them."

"I will."

"You can't drive it until we fix it. You'll do more damage," he says and walks out the door.

I meet with Duke and Charlie after school the next day. I haven't been able to concentrate since finding out they are the thieves. I've gone over and over the footage and it makes no sense. Charlie wasn't the second person in the initial stealing, yet she brought the truck back. Charlie and Duke do not hangout outside of school. So why were they together?

When they meet me at our usual table, they are uncomfortably quiet. I grill them on their math lesson waiting for them to break down and confess, but they stay strong. Duke leaves without so much as one smile or joke for the day.

"You need a ride to work?" I ask Charlie.

"If you don't mind?" she says, packing her bag up.

Maybe she'll tell me the truth on the ride over. I lead her to Nan's car, and I can tell she's searching for my truck. I tell her it's in for repairs and she doesn't even blink. This is why I don't like people, I remind myself, even though the sadness has already sunk into me. I like them. It's been such a long time since I cared about anyone the way I did with these two, and they betrayed me.

"Hey, I've got an idea," Charlie says as we pull up to her work. "Come in and let me make you a cup of coffee. On me, of course, for the tutoring." She turns to me and smiles. "Please?"

"Okay," I answer, thinking this may be her way of telling me the truth.

I follow her into the coffee house, which is somewhat empty. There are tables and lounge chairs spread out in some kind of reckless pattern. She tells me to have a seat at the coffee bar while she clocks in. I look over the leaflets on the bar of all the local bands playing. If I wasn't me, I would love to play in front of people, but such is life.

"I'm going to make you my special latte." She whips up a concoction of syrups, sugar, and coffee and froths it. "The Charlie." She pushes it to me.

I take a sip, the hot liquid burning my lips, and put it back on the bar.

"It's good, right?" She is beaming. "I can't do math, Tom, but I can do coffee."

"It's acceptable," I reply.

I can see I hurt her feelings. Her face falls flat, and she busies herself by wiping down the machine.

"I do like it," I say, wanting to make her feel better.

The bells on the door chime as someone walks in. Charlie looks up and smiles.

"Aren't you going to ask him if he wants a drink?" I ask.

"No. He's what we call the afternoon special. Get this, there's a girl who meets random dudes here and takes them somewhere for sex."

"How do you know that?" I ask.

"Same girl, different guys, almost every day. It's obvious. And they never buy a drink. Ever. Why would this girl be meeting dudes and taking them away if it wasn't sex? That's our theory anyway. Go sit in a chair and you can see firsthand. And that way you can tell us what they say to each other. There must be a code word."

Out of curiosity and wanting this conversation to stop, I grab my coffee and head to where the man is sitting. I take a table close enough to him without being obvious. I wait patiently for something to happen.

When the door opens again, everything in me ignites.

"Roxy," I say, her name escaping my lips.

She turns towards me and our eyes meet. Her eyes are the same little girl who left me all those years ago. I stand, not knowing what to say next.

She looks all grown up. Dressed in tight, black clothes and heavy eye make-up.

"Let's go," she says to the man in a rushed voice.

"Wait," I yell after her. I accidentally kick the table, spilling my Charlie special everywhere in my haste as I head to the door.

"Roxy, wait," I yell again. The man seems nervous. She whispers something to him, and he heads down the street.

"Hey, Tommy," she says, turning toward me. I'm so much taller than her. I wonder when that happened. "My friend is waiting, so I kind of have to go. But you look good."

"Hold on," I say, grabbing her small wrist. "Can we please hang out? Can we just talk? Please?"

She pauses and looks at me. Her eyes lock onto mine and seemly contemplate my question.

"Okay. Let's meet at the diner tonight. How's seven o'clock?" she says.

"That works."

"Bye, Tommy." She turns back around and walks away.

"Please don't stand me up," I yell after her.

"I won't. I promise for real."

I know she's telling me the truth. We only said promise for real when we really meant it. And we never once broke that rule. But still, I'm full of dread wondering if she'll really show, after all she broke a promise to me before. She said we'd always be best friends.

I run back into the coffee house and ask Charlie if that was the girl she was talking about. Charlie is bouncing off the walls, wanting to know how I know her. "What are the chances that Tom Moffe knows the sex girl?" she repeats over and over again.

I don't bother to answer. I have to go home. I have to get ready for Roxy.

DUKE

Football practice was a special kind of hell today with us only being one week from our first playoff game. Everyone is all business on the field, but the minute we are in the locker room all bets are off. Everyone is extra hyped and extra loud when all I want is quiet.

"Duke, what the hell happened Saturday night?" Tim says, taking his pads off. "Kristy was a drunk shit show, and Sophie spent the night babysitting her. And why did Charlie come get that kid's truck?"

"It's a long story," I say, sitting on the bench.

"I got time." He sits next to me.

I know he wants answers. He sent a ton of texts yesterday trying find out the details, but I never answered. I didn't bother talking to anyone, including my family. I just laid in my bed and pretended to do homework.

"Are you and Charlie a thing now? Kristy wouldn't shut up about you cheating on her," Smookler says.

"No. It's nothing like that. She's my friend. Just forget about it all," I say, ripping off my cleats.

"No way," Tim says.

I know he's not going to give up. This is what he does to every problem he comes across. He thinks he can break down obstacles in life like he breaks down football plays. All he needs to do is analyze it to death, and then a solution will show itself. I'm too tired to play this game with him right now.

"I ran into Charlie walking home and told her what happened. She wanted to get Tom's truck back, so we did."

"Charlie's friends with the Tom kid? Is Paige still single? She's so hot. Charlie's pretty hot, too," Tim says.

"We're both friends of his and I have no clue if Paige is single. Aren't you in love with Sophie?" I mock him.

"That ship has sailed, my friend. She was yelling at me about you screwing Kristy over and how all boys are assholes. I don't need any drama."

I watch as he says those words and know he means it. I want to ask him how he can turn off his feelings like a faucet because for the life of me I can't when it comes to Kristy.

Tim beats me getting dressed and tells me to meet him at his car. I pack all my gear away and sit alone for a minute. I should have told Tommy today. I had my chance but chickened out. I read and reread Charlie's text about how something is wrong with Tom's truck and he's driving his grandma's car around. I hope Charlie didn't say anything to him. I should be the one to say it.

"Yo, Duke," Smookler says, coming around the corner. "I'm sorry I stole your friend's truck. That really wasn't cool. I kind of feel like a jerk about it."

"Me too."

"Thanks for taking it back. I should have helped."

"Do you know how to drive a stick?" I ask.

"Yeah, I do. Did you have a problem?"

"I've never driven a stick before. I think I fucked his truck up," I say, looking away from him.

"You probably messed his clutch up."

"Is that expensive?"

"Couple hundred bucks. Tell him he can bring it to my dad's shop, and he can take a look."

"Yeah, okay, sounds good." I grab my backpack and stand.

"My dad gets the parts for cost. It could save him a lot of money. And I'll chip in." Smookler slaps my shoulders as we walk out of the locker room.

Outside, the cold air nips at my face. I see her sitting in the minivan waiting along the curb. Smookler wishes me luck and runs to Tim's car.

"Can you please get in?" she hollers out her window.

I've been putting this off. I went to extraordinary lengths to avoid her today. I even ate lunch in the hallway just to not see her. But here she is waiting, and there's nowhere to hide.

I open the passenger door and sit. She speeds off before I can fasten my seatbelt. She takes us back to the business complex we were once so happy at.

"I need to know why this is over," she says. She looks at me, her face puffy from crying, as new tears roll down her cheeks. "I love you, Duke. That's why I slept with you. I thought that meant something to you."

"It does mean something to me." My words come out too fast in almost a desperate way. "But asking me to steal Tommy's truck? I don't get it. Maybe you didn't know he was a friend, but you knew he was my tutor and I need him."

"The text was a joke. Who would have thought you guys would really do it? And, yeah it was a bad joke, but I can't be blamed for your actions. I didn't actually show up at Tommy's house and take his truck. You did. You should have said no."

It takes all my self-control not to yell back at her. I'm not used to this feeling of having to restrain my words because I've never been in a position to and I don't like it. I play with the glove box instead, opening and closing it, trying to wait out the anger.

"Say something," she demands.

"Why was it a joke to begin with? Why did you single me out? You said you were so excited to see me, then why didn't you pick the easiest, stupidest prank you could think of?" I look at her. These are the words I've been dying to say.

It's her turn to sit in silence. I resume opening and closing the glove box.

"Because I was mad at you," she finally says.

"What? Why?"

"Because you made me break up with Wyatt and that made my life hard. You didn't bother to think of that when you asked me to do it.

You only thought of yourself. But I had to break up with him so that my whole church knew and my father. Everyone was making a big deal of the two of us being together and suddenly and for no good reason, I dumped him. Now everyone feels bad for him."

"You weren't really together, and the good reason was me. I couldn't handle it. I'm not sorry about that. I don't think you could handle it if the roles were reversed. You freaked out when my friend Charlie showed up to help me with the truck."

"First of all, I was drunk, not that that's an excuse, but at least I wasn't thinking clearly. You saw how good the Wyatt plan was working and you still forced me to do it without even asking if it would cause problems for me."

"Do you hear yourself?" I yell. I can't keep the anger bottled in any longer. "It's all about you, you, you. I never came up with the Wyatt plan in the first place. You decided that this was what was best for you and never asked me. I found out through my sister."

"I did all of this for us. I did this because you are the nicest person I've ever met. You are the sweetest person I've ever met. And I'm crazy about you. I did this for love."

"You have a funny idea about what love is."

"Fuck you, Duke."

We return to silence. I slide my phone out and send a text to my sister saying I'll be a little later than usual and to let the parents know.

"I think we need a break," she says.

"Me too."

"I'm sorry I ever slept with you. I'll regret that forever."

Her words are tiny razors digging at my heart.

"Me too," I answer, getting out of the minivan.

She pulls away without so much as an offer to drive me home. I throw my backpack to the ground and sit on it. I let the tears come, and they come hard and fast, choking me from the inside out. I love her, I love her, I love her.

But I hate her more for being the person she regrets.

I don't want to go home so I walk to the coffee house instead, hoping to find Charlie.

When I swing open the shop's door, I'm hit with warmth and the strong smell of coffee. Charlie has her back to me, making someone's coffee. I hope she's still not mad at me because I could really use a friend right now.

I wait in line and order a small latte from one of her coworkers. She finally notices me when I'm waiting at the pickup counter.

"Hey, perv," she says, handing me my drink.

"Hey," I say and choke back the misery that's eating me alive. "I got your text earlier. Did he say what was wrong with his truck?"

"No. And before you ask, I didn't tell him it was us."

"Smookler thinks it's the clutch and it could be a couple hundred bucks. And before you ask, I'm going to tell Tommy it was me and give him the money to fix it."

"You're a good man, Charlie Brown. I knew you would do the right thing." She gives me her wide smile and I can't help but smile back at her.

"Listen to this," she says, coming around the counter. I know we are back to business as usual and for the first time since Saturday night, I can breathe again. She tells me all about some sex girl and how Tommy knew her and ran after this girl. "It was the most animated I've ever seen him, Duke. He looked like a totally different Tom. We have got to get to the bottom of this."

"We most definitely need to get to the bottom of this."

"Are you okay, Duke?" she asks, looking me dead in the eyes. I wonder if she can tell I've been crying.

"Never better, besides the truck thing and all," I say. She walks back to her station and gets to work on another coffee.

I can't stop thinking about Kristy. The way she looked at me as she said we needed a break, like I was pathetic. What's pathetic is the fact that we stole and broke Tommy's truck for some sort of stupid game.

I slide my phone from my pocket and send Tommy a text. I should have done this in person, but the truth is, I need to be held accountable right this minute.

THE SECONDARY WRECK: ABSOLUTION

TOMMY: AGE 17

I could hardly wait to tell my grandparents my news about finding Roxy. I leave out the horrible rumor Charlie and her coworkers are spreading about her. They are as excited for me as I am, but they do warn me to not push Roxy for answers right away. "There will be time for that later," Pop says.

"Just focus on reconnecting," Nan chimes in.

I shower and dress for the diner meeting and manage to get half of my homework done before I leave. I arrive at the diner a few minutes early and ask for a booth by the window. I hate sitting in the center of any restaurant; it makes me feel like I'm in the server's way.

I order us water and coffee not knowing what Roxy likes these days. I stare at my phone, watching the minutes pass by slowly. Maybe she's not coming after all. At ten after seven, I get a text from Duke.

It's a long story but I stole your truck Saturday night and returned it. You didn't deserve that. I have the money to fix it. I hope you'll let me explain why. You've been a good friend to me, and I didn't respect that. Sorry.

I'm dumbfounded by his honesty and by the fact that he thinks I'm a friend. I pick up the phone to answer him, but out of the corner of my eye, I spot Roxy coming through the door. I wave my hand in the air so she can see me.

She walks toward me, and I'm beginning to feel small, like the day I lost it all when she left me. She slides into the booth and smiles. "You got me coffee. Perfect." She pours three creamers and a ton of sugar in and stirs it with authority.

"How have you been?" I ask, my words feeling extra lumpy as if I am learning how to talk again.

"Good, I guess. You?"

"Okay," I answer. But what I really want to say is, *I haven't moved on from you. You broke my heart and kept all the pieces for yourself.*

"How's Pop and Nan?"

"They are good. They said to say hello to you."

"I miss them," she says and looks out to the sea of other diners.

I think she must be cold from the way she keeps tugging her sweater so the fabric is stretched past her wrist. But then I remember that this is what she always used to do when she had long sleeves on. I remember her most favorite sweatshirt was the one that had the holes in it so that she could push her thumbs through, and the sweatshirt almost became gloves.

She looks back at me and smiles. I can hardly believe that it is Roxy sitting there across the table, so grown up, so different from what I thought she'd look like. Roxy, who thought rubbing mud on her face to ward off bugs was a good idea, now is pale and caked in dark makeup and dark red lipstick.

I wonder if I turned out differently from what she expected. I watch as she continues to stir her coffee and think of the firsts we missed out on. What would it have been like for us to go to high school together? Would we have a group of friends that we always hung around, or would it have been us against the world? We could have learned to drive together. She would have absolutely loved working with Pop on that truck, though that would have made him nuts with all the questions she would have asked.

"So, how's high school? Are you the man? All the girls chasing you?" she asks.

"It's fine." I avoid the last two questions because how do you explain to someone that your presence at a place you spend a majority of time at means nothing to anyone? "How's your school?"

"I dropped out this year." Her words are short, like she would prefer no follow up questions. "Not because I'm stupid, it was just things at home got complicated."

"How are your parents?" I ask, thinking that was thoughtless of me not to ask when she brought up Nan and Pop. Every word seems so forced between us; I don't know why I was thinking that this would be easy. That we could pick up where we left off all those years ago.

"My brother and I had to move out this year."

"Oh," I say, not really knowing what to say to that.

"It's all good. Anyway, I'm taking my GED test soon, so it will be like nothing happened." Her face seems sad when she says this. She pulls extra hard on her sleeves and then crosses her arms. She looks at me like she's searching for something or someone different.

We used to talk for hours about absolutely nothing.

"Do you still play the guitar? PETA's for life?" She smiles at me, knowing this was one of our most favorite childhood fantasies. Rock stars.

"I still play. Did you ever get one yourself?"

"No."

All that foolishness of us thinking we could have been good got us here in the first place. If she hadn't been trying to save money for a stupid guitar, she would have never cut herself.

"You know your pop said something to my dad," she says, as if she could read what I was thinking. "He brought back our kitchen knives and flat out asked if someone was hurting me. He thought you were too concerned about my safety to not say anything."

"What?"

"I was sitting in the family room and heard it all. My dad kept his cool until he left, but then told me I was done being friends with you. I don't know why I'm telling you this. It was so long ago, but I guess you deserve to know why we stopped being friends. Isn't that why you wanted to meet me tonight?"

"I mean, yeah, I guess that's part of the reason why I wanted to meet you, but there're other reasons too."

"Like we could be friends again?"

"I guess so."

"I should have said something to you back then. I used to think about that a lot. But I couldn't. I was afraid if I told you the truth you would have told your pop, and then what? I begged you that day not to say something, and you did anyway."

"I didn't say anything. I just asked him to not tell your parents it was your idea," I say defensively.

"It doesn't matter now."

"It does, though. You thought you couldn't trust me, and that was never the case."

"It was my secret, Tommy. You didn't live there. You don't know how bad it was, but you thought interfering was the best solution. You made my life hell." She begins to stir the coffee that she hasn't even drunk yet.

"I didn't mean to make your life worse. I didn't even know what happened. It's not like I intentionally broke your trust."

"But it was broken."

Her phone is receiving multiple texts. She pulls it close and reads them before typing something back and then flips the phone upside down on the table.

"I have to go," she says, but doesn't get up. "Us being friends, that was a lifetime ago for me."

We lock eyes and I immediately look away. I see what she already knows. Time took us in different directions. We grew apart, and we grew up. I only know the thirteen-year-old version of her.

"I know it was a long time ago, but maybe we can try again."

"I don't think time works like that."

"I think it works any way you want it to."

"You were the best thing about growing up. Every good memory involves you. But it's different now. I'm different now."

"Can I at least give you my number? In case you change your mind?"

"Sure," she says, grabbing her phone. I tell her my number, and she sends me a text. "I've got to go."

I watch her walk away. I have waited all these years wondering if I'd ever see her again, and there she goes like none of our childhood mattered. I should have told her that I'm different now too because she walked out of my life, but that wouldn't have stopped her from doing it again now.

My grandparents are waiting eagerly for me to get home so they can ask their questions, but I'm so mad. I told Pop not to say something, and he went over that day and took away my best friend.

"Why did you say something to her parents?" I demand.

"What are you talking about?" Pop looks at me as if I were nuts.

"When she cut herself, you went over and told her parents that I thought someone was hurting her, and because of that she couldn't be friends with me."

"Wait, Tommy, I didn't say it exactly like that," Pop answers.

"Who cares how you said it? I asked you not to, but you did anyway. And you never bothered to tell me. You let me walk around here for years wondering what happened to Roxy. Why does she hate me? You knew. You knew the whole time and kept your mouth shut."

"Tommy, what was I supposed to do?"

"Not say anything like I asked."

I storm upstairs, not interested in hearing anymore. I can't help but wonder what else he decided not to tell me. Maybe things about my mom? He clearly has no sense of what *full disclosure* means. I pull out my phone and program Roxy in as a contact even though I know I won't hear from her again.

I see Duke's text and realize I never responded.

I tell him we will talk tomorrow.

Duke comes to the tutoring table, sits, and takes his books out. His jaw is tense like he's biting down on something hard. His eyes seem tired like sleep hasn't been a friend to him.

"Hey, guys," Charlie says, sitting next to Duke. "How do you know the girl?"

"We are not going to talk about her," I say, very short. She opens her mouth to say something but decides to take her books out instead.

"Tommy, can we talk about the truck? Charlie only helped me return it. She just wanted to get it back to you safe and sound."

"You didn't get it back to me safe and sound, did you? Anyway, thank you, Charlie, for helping. Duke, if you want to talk, come over to my house after practice."

"Okay, I will." He looks down at his notebook, ready to work.

DUKE

When I show up at Tommy's after practice, he is waiting for me in the driveway. Luckily for me, Mom was home, and I was able to take her car. The last time I was at his house I didn't bother looking around for obvious reasons, but now that I can take my time, I see a massive garage at the end of the driveway separate from the house.

He tells me to follow him there in a rushed voice. He keeps ahead of me like there is some kind of invisible wall separating us; I'm not about to try walking next to him. I don't know what I'm going to say to him besides the truth. It seems like a simple apology won't cut it.

"This is a cool garage," I say, following him through a side door. Tommy's truck is parked in the middle of the garage with the hood popped open like a patient waiting to go under the knife. The walls are covered with all sorts of parts. I know it's for function, but it almost has an art feel to it. The space is warm even though it's cold out.

"I guess," he answers.

There is something about him that seems more off than usual.

"I'm sorry about stealing the truck," I say. I tell him all about the night and the eventual breakup with Kristy. I can't read his face to know if he is sad or willing to forgive me. He is a stone.

I reach into my sweatpants and pull my money out. It's all waded up, so I tell him how much is there. He places the cash on the hood of the truck and counts it. I guess that's fair knowing that I can't do math really well, but still, it hurts a little that he doesn't trust me.

"Is your dad a mechanic?" I ask, realizing I know nothing about his personal life.

"No. My grandfather was, but now he's retired. This is their house," he says, making piles of the money.

"Cool. Cool. Do your mom and dad live here too?" I ask.

His quietness is killing me tonight.

"I know I really messed up here, Tommy. It was a stupid thing to do to a friend and I should have stopped it. I suck."

"Well, maybe the real issue is we're not friends, and that's why you didn't stop it."

"What?"

"You keep saying we're friends, but we're not. I just met you. I know that when it comes to Kristy, you're stupid. When it comes to math, you don't give yourself enough credit. And that's all I know. And you know even less about me."

"That's not true," I say, knowing that it is. "You have to start a friendship somewhere, so here we are."

"Look, I know you need me to keep tutoring you and I will, so stop worrying about whether or not I will help you."

"It's really not just about the tutoring."

"I have to get back inside. Nothing changes here. I'll see you tomorrow," He says, handing back some of the cash.

"You keep it for the truck." I try to push it back into his hands.

"You didn't do this alone." He walks out of the garage, and I follow. "Maybe next time, don't be such a coward."

His words dig into my ears like carpenter bees drilling into wood. I know I'm a coward, but to hear it out loud from him makes my blood run cold. This is how he sees me.

"I'm not a coward," I say.

He stops and turns around. "Coward was the wrong word." He looks right at me. "Stop being a sheep." He starts walking again and slips through the door to his house.

So that's how I'm viewed, a sheep following the herd. I slam the car door shut and jam the keys in the ignition. This was a letdown. I wanted to make peace, and all I got was called names.

Tommy's words take some kind of hold over me. It's like he gave me a map to my own life, only instead of a treasure hidden, it's some kind of release. And the thing is, I don't know how to read the fucking map. At first it seemed so simple: don't be a sheep.

But then Kristy texts. She misses me so much and she made a terrible mistake. She wants to get back together. She told her father the truth, and he is fine with us dating.

She tells the whole school the next day that we are a couple. *Look at them,* everyone says, *the star player and the head cheerleader.* Aren't we a cute couple?

This box I'm in is shrinking. It's too tight.

"Kristy." I try catching her attention before class starts. "What is going on? Why are you telling everyone we are together?"

"Because, Duke, we got into a fight. Couples do that. And I agree that making us a secret was a terrible idea. Now we are not a secret. We can be us." She leans up and kisses me on the cheek. "I love you."

I watch her walk away.

"As the world turns," Charlie says from behind me. "You got yourself an interesting girlfriend."

"She's not my girlfriend," I say.

"Given that I know all the details, way too many thanks to you, I think it's very odd that she's running around school professing her love for you. Did you say you didn't want to be with her?"

"Not exactly."

"Do you want to be with her?"

"Not exactly."

"Very vague, Duke, even for you."

"Shut up, Charlie." I loosen her schoolbag straps and laugh as she becomes unbalanced. "That never gets old!"

"You're something special." She adjusts the straps back up.

"Thanks!"

The bell summons us back to reality. "See you later," she says, running down the hallway.

Friday night lights. Playoffs. The stands are packed. Each side of the bleachers representing for their schools. Coach has been yelling at us for the last hour, getting us pumped up. The nerves are rattling me, but in a good way. I'm wound tight like a toy car; put me down and I'm off.

So, when Coach tells me I'm going to return the first kick of the game, I let out a war cry and tap my helmet. I'm ready.

The ball soars into my waiting hands and I take off. I follow the blockers down the field, my legs working like a racehorse, my vision zeroed in on the end zone. I can barely breathe when the whistles blow, indicating a touchdown. The marching band plays as the crowd sings and dances to the music.

This is playoff football. And tonight, I'm leaving it all out on the field. We are back and forth all game, in the lead and trailing, but with ten seconds left on the clock, we are down by four points and on the five-yard line.

Tim has us in the huddle and he looks at me. "All you, all day." He grabs my face mask. "Get open."

We line up on the scrimmage, my heart beating out of my chest. I look the opponent up and down, running mental footwork patterns in my head. The ball is snapped. I juke right and cut back left. I see the ball release from Tim's hand soaring at me. I catch enough of the pig skin to hold on to it. And then I feel a body hit me on my hips. I need to hold on to the ball and land on the ground, but I feel like I'm doing a cartwheel in the air. The football is still only being held onto by my fingertips when another player comes diving at me and punches the ball out.

The whistles blow. We lost. Undefeated all season and it ends with me crashing headfirst into the turf. The other team is celebrating. I watch them as I roll up onto my knees. The tears come automatically.

Smookler runs to me and pats my shoulder pads. "No one could have held onto that ball." He walks away with his head down.

I want to disappear into thin air. I don't want to walk past all these people knowing I'm the reason we lost, but almost the entire team has lined up to shake hands with the winners. A tradition that only feels respectful when you're the victor. When I join them, I am the last player in the line. I can feel the excitement pouring off the other team as we shake hands.

All the coaches and players are already jogging toward the locker room as I walk down the middle of the football field, keeping my distance from the stands. Up ahead, my dad's waiting for me.

"Are you okay?" he asks, falling in step with my stride. "That was a bad hit. It looked like you came down on your head."

"I'm fine, Dad."

"There was no way you could have held onto it."

"I don't want to talk about it," I say and trot off to the building.

Inside the locker room, everyone is mourning. Coach huddles us up and says some bullshit encouraging words that are meant to help us not beat ourselves up. But it's too late for that.

I take my time changing. No one is talking.

"I threw that ball perfectly to you," Tim finally breaks the silence. "You should have caught it."

"I tried to hold on," I say.

"We needed this win, Duke. Do you realize that we just played our last game? We needed more games for the scouts to see how good we are. My college career was riding on this," he says, throwing his helmet into the locker. The sound echoes across the room.

"It's not his fault," Smookler says.

"Whose fault is it then? Mine? Yours?"

I sit with my head down, trying to hide my tears.

"Tim, come on, he got crushed," Smookler says.

"You catch the ball, then you pull it to your body so no one can knock it loose, then you touch the turf. The end."

"You don't think I tried?" I stand.

"I get it, Duke. Playoff football is fun, but it's not necessary for you. We all know you're going to get a scholarship because I just spent the last four years making you look like a superstar. But at the end of the day, you choked and couldn't catch a simple pass."

"You're a real asshole."

"And you're not that good of a wide receiver." He slams his locker door shut and walks away.

"He's just mad right now. He didn't mean that," Smookler says, turning back to his locker.

THE SECONDARY WRECK: BIAS

TOMMY: AGE 17

I never needed social media before, mostly because I never had any friends to follow. Now it could be the one place that holds clues to Roxy's life. I make up fake accounts on all the major platforms to see if I can learn anything more about her.

She wants to say that our friendship is dead and cannot be resurrected, but I can't accept that. I didn't knowingly choose how our fate would play out; that was Pop who decided to do that. And I don't think that I should be held accountable for his actions.

She doesn't exist online; at least not under her real name. I wish my truck worked so I could just leave the house without saying anything. Downstairs, I find Nan in her sewing room and ask if I can borrow her car.

On the way out the front door, Pop reminds me that we are fixing the truck tomorrow. I haven't bothered to say much to him since the diner.

I drive past the high school and contemplate if I should go watch the game, but decide on going to the coffee house to see if Charlie is working. I drive past slowly and look through the window and find her behind the counter.

The coffee house has no customers. Charlie smiles as soon as she sees me.

"What can I get you, Tom?" She leans on the counter.

I tell her to surprise me.

"You didn't want to go to the game?" she asks.

"Not really."

"Are you still mad at Duke?" She hands me one of her creations.

"I'll be fine once I get my truck back." I take a sip of the coffee. "Wow, this is actually good."

"Oh, I see you can say nice things." She laughs, wiping up her workstation.

"Can I ask you a question?" I ask.

"Sure."

"Can we sit at a table?" I don't want her coworkers involved.

I lead us to the front of the shop and sit by the windows.

"Can you tell me more about Roxy?"

"Who's Roxy again?"

"The sex girl."

She studies my face and then says, "I don't think you need to pay for sex. If I'm honest with you, I think you're hot. You just need to talk a little more."

"I'm not trying to buy sex. She used to be my friend when we were little."

"Oh, okay, that makes me feel a little better. I don't know much about her other than what I said. Meets random dudes here and then leaves with them."

I drink the coffee, disappointed that she has nothing to really offer me.

"But you're in luck because Brian, he works the grill in the kitchen, knows her brother. I'll go get him."

She leaves me sitting with my coffee. When she comes back, she is followed by a tall, very skinny, kid.

He sits across from me and sips from a cup of ice water.

"How do you know Roxy?" I ask him.

"I don't really know her, but I was good friends with her brother in high school. I don't talk to him now, but I know he lives here in the borough. I sort of avoid him at all costs. Dude is fucked up."

"What do you mean?" I think of the Jack I knew. He was bigger than us and definitely a jerk, always making fun of me and Roxy, calling us babies when we played.

"He was just always getting into real trouble. I cut ties with him after he got arrested for his DUI. I tried stopping him from driving home and he sucker punched me for the keys. I kind of lost respect for him after that."

"Do you think that she is really..." I pause, trying to find the right way to phrase my question.

"Do I think she sells herself?" he says.

"Yes. Do you think that?"

"That's what I hear. Some of my friends still talk to him. That's what I'm saying, dude is messed up. How could he sit back and let that happen? It's gross."

I lean back in my chair and let out a sigh. I want to be sick thinking about Roxy selling her body for money. My Roxy. "Do you know where they live?"

"Listen, I wouldn't get involved if I were you. He doesn't care about anything. That's my advice and now I must go clean up back there so I can get home already."

He stands and stretches. I stare out the window, thinking about how innocent we all were back then and wonder what could make her do this. Why would Roxy, the most confident girl I've ever met, be willing to trade off her body for money?

"They live above the Tap Room," he says and walks back to the kitchen.

"Are you okay?" Charlie asks.

"I'm fine," I say. "Thanks for the coffee."

Out in the street, I find my bearings. It takes a minute to remember which direction the Tap Room is in, but once I think of it, I start walking the short walk there. The street is quiet tonight. It's never really busy during cold weather. I walk around the back of the building, hoping to find an entrance to the apartment.

"Tommy, what are you doing here?" Roxy says. She's leaning against a car.

"I need to know," I say, walking toward her.

"Know what?" She has a confused look on her face.

"The rumors about you, are they true?"

"What rumors?"

"That you have sex with men for money."

"Tommy, it's really none of your business."

"It is my business. You are my family. I didn't pick losing you, Roxy," I yell at her.

"Don't get loud," she warns.

"I have spent the last four years being quiet. Not talking to anyone because I couldn't care about what they had to say because they weren't you. You left me."

"I don't think I really had anything to do with that."

"I lost my best friend right after I lost my mother. It was like you died too, Roxy. And because of that, I also died. You want to blame me for breaking our trust, but you broke it too. We are both at fault here."

"Do you feel better now that you came and said what you had to?"

"No. Because I need to know if it's true."

"What difference does it make?" she asks.

"Because I can help you."

"I'm not a little kid anymore. I don't need help. I don't need Tommy to come save me. What if it is true? What if I sell myself? You know nothing about my life." Her words are full of bitterness.

"I don't understand, why won't you let me help you?" I say, just above a whisper. I can feel myself slipping inwards, finding shelter from her truth. She sees it too.

"I don't want your help. What don't you get?"

"But," I say, trying to find the right words.

"You can't fix this. No one can. Things got really bad after I moved. My mom left my dad. My dad left the family. My grandmother died, leaving us homeless. I have no clue where my parents are, and I don't care to find them." She sighs. "You can believe in whatever version of me that makes you happy, but at the end of the day, you're not paying my bills. I am."

"All I'm saying is you don't have to do this. You can come live with me. Your brother can fend for himself," I say, still trying to pull her back to me.

"You of all people know that life isn't fair or kind, but we have to live it anyway. I'm living mine, Tommy. Why don't you go live yours?" She walks past me and up a rickety staircase to the second floor.

The next morning, I wake early to Pop knocking on my door to remind me that it's time to work on the truck. I slowly shake the sleep off, fighting off the ghost of last night's encounter with Roxy. Downstairs, I fumble around getting my coffee together in the thermos, all the while Nan watches, perched on top of the kitchen stool.

"He loves you, Tommy," she says.

"I know that," I mumble, not wanting to show her disrespect.

"The thing about us old people," she says, waiting for me to make eye contact, "is that we are running out of time. Not that your pop is sick, I'm just saying we have less time here on earth than you do. And we lived a whole lot longer, meaning that we have made far more mistakes than you can possibly know. We aren't perfect. No human is. Your pop wasn't trying to hurt you or Roxy. And he should have told you the truth all those years ago, but what you'll discover in life is that sometimes your actions, even with good intent, will have ripple effects that you didn't plan on, and sometimes those ripples are really hard to confess to when you know it will hurt the person you love the most. Can you see it that way? That he didn't mean to take Roxy away?"

"I don't know."

"I understand. Just think about what I said. Can you do that for me?" She glances away, toward the window.

"I can."

I take my coffee and head for the garage, stopping to look at Roxy's old house. Maybe there was no way for anyone to save her all those years ago. Or perhaps that is the version of me that wanted to ignore all the warnings signs and red flags that I overlooked. My job was to make her smile and be her friend, and I did that well.

But there is also that little version of me that sat idle while my mom got high and knew when she needed a hug because her body hurt and knew when to hide because the angry, withdrawn Mom would soon strike.

I've always known how to react. I've never known how to act.

Truth is a cyanide pill to illusion.

It wakes the subconscious like a clap of thunder. I remember Pop in the hospital all those years ago when Mom almost died on the deck. I hid in the closet of the office the police brought me to. I was so scared. I lost all my words. I couldn't have one more person look at me. I killed Mom. I couldn't protect her.

Pop crawled in the closet and sat with me, knees bent all the way to his chest. We both didn't fit in the space, but he contorted his body, determined not to let me sit alone. He didn't say a word. After some time, he managed to maneuver his arm around my little body, then he said, his breath warm on my forehead, "I've got you."

And he has. He has always protected me since that day.

DUKE

I watch the sun rise and feel lost as to what to do today. Saturdays are gym days with Smookler and Tim, but I already know that isn't happening. I check my phone, hoping Kristy would have texted more, but she's gone silent. She only sent me a heart and a sad face emoji since last night's loss.

I was hoping that she would have waited and taken me home after the game, but she was nowhere to be found. Thank God Jayla stuck around to see if I was okay because she was at least able to give me a lift home.

After I brushed my teeth and went into my room, she came in and laid at the foot of my bed. It was the first time in a long time I cried in front of her. She was my float in the deep blue sea, just witnessing the wreck without any words. Larry was right, family loves you best even when you fuck up and lose the game.

By ten in the morning, I'm already bored. I ask my mom for her car for a couple hours to study with Tommy. I don't want to tell her the truth, which is that if I don't do something, I'm going to lose it. Maybe she already knows that because she hands the keys over without even asking any follow-up questions like she usually does.

I cruise the streets endlessly, listening to loud music and then turning the volume all the way down. Up and down. Road after road. In my mind, I see the football. I feel it in my hands. I play it over and over again until I catch it and we win. But that is a lie. We lost. The end.

I eventually find myself parked out front of Tommy's house. Even though it's chilly out, the garage door is open, and I can see an old man and Tommy looking under the truck that is on a lift.

I jump out of my car and walk toward them.

"Hey, guys, can you use a hand?" I say, trying not to sound too deflated.

"What are you doing here?" Tommy asks, popping his head up from under the truck.

"I just want to help," I say in an almost begging voice.

"The more the merrier," the old man says. "I'm Tommy's grandfather, Pop." He sticks his greasy glove out to me. "Sorry, habit." He pulls his hand back. "What do you know about cars?"

"Absolutely nothing," I answer. "I only know football."

"Doesn't matter," he says, leaning back over the hood. "Did you guys win last night? Big playoff game, right?"

"We lost," I say, fighting back the tears that seem never ending.

"Tough break. You guys played well this year," he says. "Now if you look under here, what we're going to be doing is removing the transaxle and then unbolting the engine mount so we can remove and replace the clutch."

I look at Tommy to see if he is bothered by me being here. He doesn't seem to care one way or another. Instead, he digs into a box of latex gloves and hands me a pair.

Tommy and I do as we are told by Pop and work diligently for two hours. Pop explains, in full detail, every step as we are doing them, and I realize why Tommy is such a good teacher—he learned from his grandfather how to make something complicated easy to understand. At some point, Tommy's grandma comes out to check on the status of the truck.

I introduce myself to her because Tommy is way under the truck. She tells us that since we're working so hard, she was thinking pizza for lunch.

When the delivery man arrives with the pies, I am drenched in sweat and so hungry I know I'm going to have to use extra control not to eat an entire pizza myself. I'm expecting Tommy's parents to join us, but it turns out to be just the four of us.

All of us eat lunch in the garage because we are too dirty to come in the house.

"How do you know Tommy?" she asks.

"He's my math tutor," I answer, slightly upset that Tommy must never talk about me. "He's the best. He tutors our other friend, Charlie, and both of us now have a solid B in that class."

"Very good. Tommy is a smart kid. Princeton bound," she says, smiling at me.

"Really? I didn't know you were applying there."

"We are all proud of him," she says, looking at Tommy.

"How about you, Duke? Are you heading off to college?" Pop asks.

"I'll go to whatever school offers the most scholarship money."

"You're not going to choose a school? You're just going to go to the highest bidder?" Tommy asks.

"Pretty much. College is expensive and my parents are very honest. I need the money, or I can't go."

"But don't you have a school you really want to go to?" Tommy's face is somewhere between disgust and bewilderment.

"Temple University," I say between bites. "But really, any school is fine by me."

We all continue to eat pizza, the buzz of the afternoon floating by us. It has turned out to be a nice, warm fall day. I watch as the leaves drop from the trees in their front yard.

I look over at the door that leads out of the garage and notice a growth chart with the names "Tommy" and "Roxy" written in black ink with their ages written next to them.

"Who is Roxy?" I ask.

For a moment, the garage grows very tight, like all the air was sucked out.

"That was Tommy's childhood friend," Pop says.

"She moved away," his grandma adds quickly.

Tommy remains a stone.

"Oh wait, is that the girl from the coffee house?" I ask, looking at him.

"Yes," he answers.

"Nice. So, you guys reconnected, right?" I push on.

"No, Duke, she doesn't want to be friends." He drops the crust on his plate in a way that makes me realize I should shut my mouth.

We get back to work for another hour before I have to leave. I tell them how much fun I had learning how to fix the truck.

After I explain to my parents why I'm covered in grease and dirt, I take a long, hot shower. Kristy has yet to respond to any of my texts asking her to go on a date to dinner and a movie.

I break down and finally call her.

"Did you get my texts?" I ask.

"I did."

"Are you free tonight?"

"Actually, Sophie is having a party."

"Okay, we can do that instead," I say, feeling the dread of seeing the football team wash over me.

"Well, about that. You're not really invited."

Silence.

"It's just that Tim is still mad, and he and Sophie sort of have that weird 'will they or won't they hook up' vibe. It's not a big deal."

"It is a big deal," I say, the anger burning me alive.

"It's not. This will blow over between you two."

"And you'd rather go to the party than hang out with me?"

"It's our last cheerleader and football player party of high school, Duke. I can't miss it. I'm the captain."

"That means nothing. I'm your boyfriend. You should want to hang out with me."

"I'm not getting into this with you. I'm going to the party."

"Good for you. Go single because this between us is over."

I hang up and throw the phone to the carpet. I expect to hear texts come through with her calling me an asshole, but none arrive.

"Mom," I yell out my bedroom door.

"Why are you yelling so loud?" she says, coming out of her bedroom.

"I need the car again."

"Why are you so mad?" she asks, putting her hand on my arm.

"I can't talk about it."

"You're going to have to try if you want my car. I'm not letting you drive mad."

"Oh my god, Mom!"

"Duke, you need to calm down."

"What's going on back here?" Dad asks, walking down the hall.

"I'm mad," I yell.

"We can see that." Dad takes my arm and guides me into my room. He tells Mom he's got this and shuts the door.

"Football?" he asks, sitting on the bed.

"Life," I answer, pulling out my desk chair. "I don't want to talk about it, Dad. I just want to take a drive and be alone."

"Makes sense. I like to do the same thing when I'm pissed off too. I just need to know one thing: are you blaming yourself? Because the ball was thrown out of your reach. There was nothing you could do about that."

"I'm just mad at everything, Dad. I really don't want to talk now."

"Okay, here's the deal. I'm going to give you my car keys and we are going to tell your mom that everything is fine. You are going to walk out of this room like a normal teenager and not like the Hulk. Can you do that?"

"Yes."

I'm out the door before Mom can play detective. Here I go again, driving nowhere, just endless streets until I pass the coffee house.

When I get to the counter, I order coffee and two muffins because I'm starving.

"Last night Tommy stopped in and now you. This is a great weekend," Charlie says, handing my order to me.

"Why did Tommy stop in?"

"To ask questions about a friend of his, Roxy. Who, in my opinion, Tommy should stay away from, but what do I know? I wonder if he found her last night."

"He didn't mention it when I saw him today. He did say she didn't want to be friends."

"Interesting. I have to get back to work."

"Hey, if she comes in, let me know," I say, walking to an empty table.

The coffee house is full so I can people watch and sort of distract my mind. I'm fighting the urge to crash Sophie's party and tell Tim and Kristy what pieces of shit I think they are. All these years of being a team and brothers and they disown me because of dropping an uncatchable ball. I should be at that party tonight.

I barely hear Charlie next to me telling me that Roxy just walked in, but I do. I see her dressed in black, skin and bone, pale like a vampire. I remember the flash of disappointment on Tommy's face when he said she didn't want to be friends and feel that rejection all the way to the bone.

People have a lot of nerve these days.

She is already walking back out the door, but I don't skip a beat and I'm a hell of a lot faster than she is.

"Roxy, stop," I say, walking behind her. "We need to talk."

THE SECONDARY WRECK: MEMORIES

TOMMY: AGE 17

I've kept a Roxy box all these years stashed in my closet, full of summer bucket lists, artwork, notebooks full of lyrics and stories, pictures, and of course her Christmas gift I never got to give her. I unfold the shirt and run my fingers over the lettering, feeling the years weigh me down.

I know that part of growing up is growing too big for your childhood beliefs. We grow out of all the magical lure of gifts under the tree by a strange man in a red suit and other weird tall tales we are subscribed to as a child. That is part of the contract of being alive. We have to grow up. And we want to.

But there are side effects that never get brought up by those who have lived long enough to know the pitfalls that lay waiting for us. One of them being that the person who you thought would be your friend for life will also outgrow you.

Roxy could still want to be my friend, but the truth is I hold no value to her in her life anymore. I'm irrelevant. I've played my part and every new scene needs a cast change. I can't possibly think that there was a placeholder waiting for me to finally turn back up and resume my position in her life.

The worst part of this revelation is that I've been living my life as a nobody, hoping to remain the same for when we did meet up again because in my mind, I always found her. She always loved me. I didn't change for her. I stopped living.

For the first time since she vanished, I feel the hurt she left in her wake. And I'm mad. Not only at her, but at myself for thinking any of this mattered.

I look at the photographs of me and her and still see myself even though my physical appearance has changed. I'm still that little boy afraid of what the world would take from him.

And who has she become? I touch her face in the photograph. She dreamed so big back then. Right before the incident, she talked excessively about how we would go off to college together. I remember her sitting on my bed, holding the guitar in her lap, talking about how much she loved Harvard. She said the buildings there were so old they reminded her of castles. Of course, she only really knew this from watching a movie, but that didn't matter. What mattered was she desperately needed to get accepted into the university. When I tried to explain that it was an Ivy League college and it would be extremely hard to get in, she waved my words off with the fling of her wrist. She never did mind a challenge. I'd rather reach for things I knew I could get because the fear of failing never did sit well with me. But the only fear I had in that moment was that she was going to leave me behind. She was smarter than me, so that meant I had to study twice as hard if I was going to follow her. And I knew the thing about Roxy was that once her mind was made up, there was no going back.

Now she's selling herself to make rent, and there is nothing I can do but know the truth. That and head off to the Ivy League college we both should be going to. She would probably be disappointed that I never did apply to Harvard because that felt like a betrayal in the highest regard.

It is a fool's heart who believes they can shape the world for another when they can barely shape their own. And I have spent my entire life playing the fool.

"Knock, knock," Pop says, coming through the door. "Are you hungry?"

He looks to the floor at the complete mess I've made dumping the Roxy box out. He bends over and picks up a picture.

"I remember this day," he says, sitting next to me. He stares at me on my bike and Roxy standing next to me. "She couldn't believe you didn't know how to ride a bike. Remember? She kept repeating it the whole time I built that bike like you were going to suddenly realize that you knew how to ride."

"She was so annoying," I say and smile, feeling the tears pooling in my eyes. "She laughed at me when I asked you to put training wheels on."

"Yeah, but she was also a good teacher."

"Are you kidding? She told me she had the back of the bike and somewhere along the line, she let go and I freaked out and crashed."

"That's how you teach someone to ride a bike."

I sit back and think about how close this is to real life. How she held onto me as I came to live with Pop and Nan, how she never left my side when my mom died, and when everything finally felt automatic in my life, she let go.

"I just wish we could be friends now, but I guess she's moved on with her life." I pick up another photograph of us out in the garden with Nan.

"Life is such a long journey, Tommy. Never think that you know the outcome because the truth is, we never do. We guess, and we get it wrong ninety percent of the time. That's why everyone always talks about being in the moment, because at that end of the day, that's all we really have."

"But then why plan?" I question his logic.

"Plans are like blueprints. And the great thing about blueprints is that the design can still change. The only thing that is permanent is the foundation, and even that can be torn up and poured again."

"Okay," I say, looking at another photograph of Roxy dressed as a pirate. It wasn't even Halloween. It was the middle of summer. She claimed she was trying out a new idea for themed dinner parties only she didn't tell us she was dressing up, which made Nan laugh so hard she had to run to the bathroom yelling she was going to pee herself. Roxy always loved it when she could get Nan laughing like that. "Let's take your blueprint analogy one step further. How do we know if we are building the right structure? How do you know before it's too late?"

"It's in the moments we have. That's what I'm saying. You can feel this moment here. Are you happy? Is there something you're not doing that you want to? Moments are like our guides if you're willing to listen to them."

"Well, I'm not happy and my guide seems to be on a break," I say, scooping up the Roxy stuff putting it back into the box.

"I'm sorry I didn't tell you the truth," he says.

"I know you are, Pop."

"I wish I told you."

"I know."

I drag the box back to the closet. It doesn't seem right to throw out all those memories and erase whatever happiness I did have all those years ago. Maybe in a few years I won't feel as though they are some kind of extension of me, but for now they need to live jammed in the way back, out of sight. Downstairs, I join them for dinner, all the while thinking of the Christmas gift. Even though I think the guide thing is crap, I kind of think it wants me to give Roxy her Christmas present. Or maybe that's me just looking for closure.

"I'm going to take the truck out for a ride. Is that okay?" I ask, putting the dishes in the dishwasher.

"The truck is good now. I liked that Duke kid. He seems nice," Pop says, handing me a plate.

"Yea, he's not so bad." I smile thinking of him wrenching with Pop and me. It takes a lot of courage to fix what you broke in someone's life. Maybe he's not the sheep I thought he was.

Upstairs, I spray Roxy's shirt with some wrinkle release spray Nan thought was important for me to have, and fold the shirt nicely. I walk over to my guitars and pick up the one Roxy and I first learned how to play. She was so desperate to get her own. It was all she ever talked about.

I take out my cloth and wax and give the guitar a nice cleaning. I play a couple of Roxy's favorite songs, running my fingers up and down the fret board. There's a part of letting this guitar go that is so sad, and there's a part that is so freeing. She should have this. I grab some of my extra strings in case I actually find her and if she wants me to, I can restring this for her.

I carry all of it downstairs with me. Nan and Pop are already sitting on the couch, watching the television.

"I'm going to give this stuff to Roxy," I say. "Is that okay with you?"

"Why wouldn't it be okay? It's yours to give away," Nan says.

"Just checking."

"Good luck," Pop says.

"Okay," I say and leave.

The truck rumbles to life and I sit for a minute feeling the engine idle, happy to have it back. I hope Roxy is home, but I have no clue what she does on a Saturday night. And it's already getting late. She could be out, and this could be a fail. I can't leave all this by her back door because I want to make sure she gets it. This is a stupid idea. Maybe I should just drive around for a while and then go back home.

After all, I know she won't be thrilled to see me, but I'll promise her I won't come around after tonight.

DUKE

Roxy gives me a side glance but keeps walking. She tightens her grip on her purse. She's picking up her speed but not putting any distance between us as I slowly jog toward her.

"Hey, you got a second?" I yell after her again. "I just want to talk to you about Tommy for a minute. Please."

She slows her pace and says, "Who the hell are you?"

"I'm no one. Okay, that's not true, I'm Duke, Tommy's friend."

"Good for you."

I catch up to her and we walk side by side.

"It would be nice if you'd stop following me," she says.

"Just stop walking and let me talk. It won't take long."

"Why would I do that? I told Tommy to leave me alone. Did he send you to stalk me?"

"Whoa, I'm not stalking. I called out your name and asked you to talk. These are not stalking qualities. Tommy has no clue I'm here and if he did, he would be pissed at me."

"Then why are you here?"

"Because Tommy is a good person. He's honest. He keeps his word. And I just don't know why you don't want to be friends with a person like that. They're hard to come by."

"Well, I'm glad you found him, but I don't see why any of this matters to me."

"Because he seems sad about you and that matters to me."

"What do you even know about me and Tommy?" She suddenly stops. I can see her shivering. She should be wearing a coat instead of the little black sweater that I can practically see through. If I had my coat, I would offer it to her even though I'm pretty sure she would rather freeze to death than take anything from me.

"Nothing. He doesn't talk about it. He doesn't talk about anything for that matter. It's impossible to get to know him."

"I thought you said you were friends."

"We are. I just met him a couple of months ago even though we've been in the same school forever." The words sound so stupid coming out of my mouth. "It's a big school," I add, trying to make myself feel better.

She begins to walk. "My and Tommy's past is a complicated subject built on bad family circumstances and proximity. We had each other because we lived next door. I moved, and the friendship ended. This shit happens every day. So, I hope that clears it up for you because you obviously have no clue what you're talking about."

"Yes, I do know what I'm talking about. Everyone walks around telling you what you want to hear, what you want to believe, but the moment life gets tough they vanish. Except for Tommy. Even though I messed up, he accepted me for me. And you may not think that is a good quality for a friend, but I happen to think it's the best."

"Look, I don't know you, Duke, I don't want to know you, so how about we just end this awkward conversation."

"I think if you could just give him a chance, you'd see he's worth it."

"Goodnight, Duke."

"Wait, I have one more question, where are Tommy's parents? He never talks about them and I've never seen them around."

She stops walking. Something I said bothered her. She looks past me and then back at me as if deciding something.

"That's because his mom is dead, and he doesn't know who his father is."

"Oh, okay." I'm taken back by her words. She looks at me and her face softens just a bit.

"She was a drug addict most of Tommy's life, but then she cleaned herself up and was killed in a car accident when we were twelve."

"Wow," I say, thinking of Tommy. I always knew there was something about his quietness that seemed like a big deal.

"Tommy is a great person, don't get me wrong," she says, crossing her arms. "But he has the propensity to try and fix any wounded person he comes across, and at this point in my life, I don't want to be saved. And he doesn't understand that. There you have it. The truth."

We continue to walk down the street. I feel sick to my stomach thinking of all the times I tried to get Tommy to talk about his mom and being pissed that he was always quiet. Why didn't I think to shut my mouth?

"I was trying to do something nice for him by getting you to reconsider being friends. Have a good night," I say and turn back towards the coffee house.

Back inside, I sit at the table where my half-eaten muffin waits for me. The coffee house thins out, so it's just me and the staff in the building. I still can't bring myself to eat the last little bit of the muffin, so I ball it up and toss it in the trash.

Charlie comes out from behind the counter and begins wiping down the empty tables. She asks about what I said to Roxy and I fill her in on what just happened and about the party at Sophie's that I wasn't invited to.

"Are you really done with her now?" she asks, resuming wiping down the tables, ignoring the Tommy's-mom-dying part.

"Yes, I'm really done with Kristy."

"Good."

"I want to crash the party though. I want to tell those assholes off."

"Let's go then."

Charlie finishes her shift and we wait while the manager locks up the shop.

"You know Tim still has the biggest crush on Paige?" I say as we pull away.

"I can't wait to tell her that!" she says, laughing.

"Why is that so funny?"

"Because he was a total douche bag to her. He was always blowing her off and making her feel less than because she was artsy. She couldn't stand him."

"He is a douche bag."

I pull up to Sophie's house, remembering the last time I was here with Charlie. I think about what a different story it would be if we had won the game. I would be in there with Kristy, but instead I'm out here and this feels right. I almost hate the person I would have been in there. Walking around drinking and thinking these people were my friends when really, they weren't.

"I can't go in," I finally say and recline my seat back.

"Well, it was sort of a bad idea anyway." She reclines her seat back too.

"A terrible idea." I pull the sunroof open so we can look out into the sky that seems endless.

"Let's play a game." Her voice is full of excitement.

"Okay. What's the game?"

"We say what we would have wanted to say if we went into the party."

"Ladies and gentlemen, you are all assholes," I say, feeling the bitterness ooze from my lips.

"Okay. Good start. I'd say, excuse me, and keep in mind I'd be standing on a chair so everyone could see me. And then I'd say, my friend Duke and I just came to say that it's real fucked up that he wasn't invited tonight. He played every game to win. He thought you guys understood that, but clearly you must have forgot. Anyway, I, for one, am super grateful that he dumped you, Kristy, because you two were annoying. And I'm also glad that I got to know him because he's a pretty cool guy."

"I am a pretty cool guy," I say, turning my face toward her.

"And then what else would you say?" She looks at me. "Because I'm pretty sure that is not what you would say in my version of the story."

"Oh yeah? What would I say?"

"First, you would say thank you, Charlie, you're pretty awesome too. And then you'd say how crushed your feelings are. How sad it makes you that they could be this mad at you for not catching the ball. That all these years mattered to you and so did their friendship."

"Charlie, you are awesome. You are not as cool as me."

"Duke!"

"I am sad. Sad that all of this is over. High school and all. But I'm also mad. I'm a mixed bag of feelings."

"It is really messed up."

I close my eyes and think of when I was little and everything still felt right. Every memory I have growing up is of me and Tim playing ball. All the sleepovers we had playing video games, arguing about who got to be the Eagles. What a dick.

"And then there's Kristy," Charlie says, bringing me back to reality.

"She's easy. I would say to her, you're just a sad little girl who only knows how to use people."

"Good one."

We sit in the car for a long time in silence. My shifting thoughts between those assholes in the house and Tommy.

"I can't believe Tommy's mom was a drug addict," I say, mostly to myself.

"I can't believe she told you that. If that were me, I think I would have kept that one a secret."

"I'm glad she did. In a way, it kind of explains Tommy. Why he's so lonely."

"You think Tom is lonely? I don't think that at all." She opens her eyes and looks at me. "I think he's content with who he is. He doesn't need people to make him happy."

"We all need people. I don't know what I'd do without my family. Shit, just a few days ago I wouldn't know what to do without those assholes at the party."

"Maybe Tom's built differently," she answers.

"Don't you need people?" I ask, feeling a little vulnerable.

"Of course, I do. I was just saying that not everyone is the same. We all have different needs. Like you needed to be the star of the football team and I needed my best friends to make funny videos with me. We tend to gravitate to what we want and who we want to be around. Maybe Tom doesn't want to be around people."

"Or maybe he doesn't know how?" I say.

"Maybe," she answers. "I think he likes us, even after the truck thing, so maybe we're both wrong."

"I hope so."

"Remember when you chased a girl down the street tonight? You are such a perv. You see it now, right?"

"Shut up."

We settle back in the comfortable silence; the only sound is the heater humming while blowing out warm air.

"Charlie?"

"Present."

"Thanks for fake crashing this party with me."

"Duke?"

"Present."

"Thanks for giving me a ride home."

"Who said I was giving you a ride home?" I raise my seat and put the car in drive.

THE SECONDARY WRECK: GOODBYES

TOMMY: AGE 17

I sit in the back lot of her building, wondering if I have enough balls to actually climb her staircase and knock on the door. The guitar and shirt sit next to me in the passenger seat.

In the world of me and Roxy, she was always the braver one of us. She didn't hesitate or think of consequences, she just did and dealt with the aftermath later. I have always been much more careful than her. We balanced each other out in that way.

The summer before she moved, she came up with a plan to sneak out of our houses after everyone fell asleep. I was a hard no, but like Roxy always did, she wore me down. She would talk endlessly about it and she even drew escape plans from our bedrooms and where we would meet.

I said to her, "All this for what? What could we possibly do in the middle of the night?"

She said, face as serious as it could be, "Ride our bikes." Night riding, as she called it.

On her illustration, I wrote a list of things that could possibly happen to us along with the grounding we would receive.

She drew a man with a penis. She asked me what was missing; she didn't wait for my response before saying balls. The balls were missing.

That's how she got me to sneak out of my house and have the best night ever riding bikes under the moonlit night.

Without any more overthinking, I climb out of my truck and head up the rickety steps to her house. I knock lightly and almost run away.

She opens the door and already has a look of disgust on her face. She's wearing a set of flannel pajamas with ducks printed on them.

"I just came to give these to you and then I'm leaving." I hold up the guitar.

Her eyes go huge like they used to when she came up with the next best thing before fading back to the new Roxy look. The one in which I am insignificant and wasting her time.

"I can't take that from you," she says, her voice more welcoming than it was last night.

"I have another one that I play on. I want you to have this."

"Come in, you're letting the cold air get in." She opens the door wide, inviting me in.

I step into a tiny kitchen. There's barely enough room for us to be standing in it and having the door open. I lean against the stove as she closes the door. I look around at the dated appliances and I'm instantly brought back to all the apartments I lived in with Mom. She walks past me without speaking.

I follow her down a narrow hallway.

"That's my brother's room," she says, pointing to a closed door. "That's the bathroom, and this is my room."

I look in for a moment but don't take much in. Everything is becoming closed in and I know I have to breathe deep breaths and this will pass. We dead end into the living room. There are two mismatched sofas, one against a bare wall, and the other beneath a giant bay window. Two lamps, one in each corner, give the room a soft glow.

"Your place is nice," I say, sitting d on the closest sofa. "If you have a minute, I would like to change the strings on the guitar so it sounds better when you play."

"You really don't have to give it to me."

"It feels right," I say, digging the strings out of my pocket. "It belongs to you as much as it belongs me."

"What's that on your lap?"

"It's an old Christmas gift I want you to have. It's kind of silly, but I've kept it all these years." I hand her the shirt and watch as she reads it.

"The PETA's," she says and looks at me. "It's not kind of silly, I love it."

I continue taking all the strings off and placing them on the coffee table. She holds the shirt against her like a blanket and watches me. The space between the years settles around us. What can you talk about when there is no future and a fractured past? Nothing.

"I got all this furniture at a thrift shop. I think I spent less than two hundred dollars in this room. Not bad, right?" she says, looking at the pile of discarded strings on the coffee table.

"I think it looks great. You did a good job."

"I need to get something for the walls. It seems a little empty in here," she adds.

"Remember the summer Pop got us that big roll of paper?" I say, putting the E string on.

"Oh my god! I do. We spread it out and basically threw paint at it thinking we were the next big thing in the art world." She laughs.

"Surprisingly, it looked good. That's what you need for the wall behind me."

"We basically painted half of your yard that day. Your grandparents were so cool. They let us do whatever we wanted."

"They did," I say, thinking back to those days.

"The good old days," she says, and drifts off to space. I continue with my task, trying not to think of the things I wish I could say to her.

"You've gotten really good at that," she says. "I remember when we first started out you were afraid to change the strings because you thought they were going to snap off and cut you."

"I remember that," I answer. "It's second nature now. But for the record, I have cut myself." I put the last string on and begin tuning it.

"That sounds so good. I can't wait to play," she says, her face reminding me of little Roxy, so happy.

"You're going to sound great when you knock the dust off your playing. You got really good before you left."

"Almost as good as you."

"If you had your own guitar, you would have been better than me."

"Play me a song," she says.

I start playing and eventually begin to play the songs we loved the most all those years ago. She sings along with me, all those years melt away and it's just me and her, pure and unscathed by the world.

We stop singing and I hand her the guitar. She rests it in her arms and starts placing her fingers on the frets. I remind her again that it will all come back to her once she plays for a while.

"It's getting late," I say, not wanting to overstay my welcome.

"I'm sorry I was such a bitch to you."

"It's okay."

"It's really not. You came over here and gave me back some childhood possessions. I barely have any of those. You can't know what this means to me."

"I'm glad you like them." I look at her and take it all in.

"My life isn't as bad as it seems." She places the guitar next to her on the sofa.

"Okay," I answer, not wanting to add anymore words. I want the world to stop right here in this fleeting moment. Please pause. Here is where I feel whole again. Home again.

"Everything is temporary. Not that I have to justify myself to you."

"You don't."

"But I do want to. Isn't that funny?"

"I wasn't trying to judge you."

"I know."

We sit in silence.

"I have everything under control. I'm not going to waste my life in this apartment. And I really don't want you to think I'm not thankful for your kindness. Because I am."

"I was always the nicer one out of us," I say, offering a small smile.

"Keep telling yourself that," she says with a laugh. Outside the window, voices float up to us from the street. Life goes on even as the time left between us fades away.

"I'm sorry for it all. For the way things turned out."

"I know."

"If you ever need anything, just let me know. You'll always be my friend."

Her eyes drift away from me and I know I've lost her again. Maybe it would have been better to have never found her again, because losing her a second time feels like I'm being crushed by the weight of a tractor trailer. It's too hard to let her go again, but I know I have to.

"Okay, well I'll see you around," I say, standing, hoping she'll ask me to sit back down and stay for a while. When she doesn't say a word, I leave, walking back through the narrow hallway and into the kitchen. I'm about to open the door when I hear her running toward me.

I turn in enough time to receive her hug. She holds on tight and we stay locked together for what feels like an eternity. I want to pull her back when she lets go.

"See you later, alligator," she says.

"In a while, crocodile," I say back.

She grabs my hand and squeezes, and I squeeze back.

Outside, the cool air does nothing for my racing heart. I know I'm having a full-blown panic attack; I've had these before. I need to sit for a minute to calm myself down, but there are no seats. I think about knocking and asking to come back inside until it passes, but my legs feel like Jell-O, barely able to hold my weight up. I lean against the wood railing, fighting the urge the pass out. *Deep breaths,* I remind myself. In and out. I am safe. My body starts to settle when I hear a crack in the wood and a little give.

I try my hardest to lean forward to offset the weightlessness I suddenly feel where my body was leaning, but it's too late. I am falling to the ground.

I come to for a moment. Roxy. She's here. I hurt so bad. It's the worst headache ever. I close my eyes and fade into the blackness.

DUKE

After I drop Charlie off at her house, I take the long way home, hoping to kill enough time so that Mom and Dad are in bed. When I pull into the driveway, I notice the back lights are still on. Larry must have fallen asleep out there again.

I throw Dad's keys in the bowl in the foyer that collects all things found in pockets. In the kitchen, I poke around the fridge for leftovers; those muffins were not enough to eat.

"You feeling better?" Dad asks, coming into the kitchen, looking like he just woke up.

"Yeah. Thank you for letting me take the car." I grab a piece of chicken Mom cooked and eat it cold.

Dad looks out the sliding door. "He's asleep again."

"I'll get him. Go back to bed."

"Thanks," he says, shuffling back out of the kitchen.

I finish the chicken and grab an iced tea before going out to wake Larry. I sit in the chair next to him and let the cool air wash over me.

In the semi-darkness, I allow the tears to come again. I can't seem to shake them. Betrayal is the worst kind of wound because it never lets your mind rest. It's like being stuck in a spider web, and every new direction I try to move my mind into, the web of deceit sticks anyway. It's almost useless to try and fight it.

"Hey, little man," Larry says, adjusting his body on the chair. "What's with you?"

"I had a crap day."

"Oh, those are the worst."

"Sure are."

"Still upset about the game?"

"That and it turns out my friends are assholes."

"Friends can be like that."

"I guess I thought they weren't."

"It happens."

"I made a mistake. I made many mistakes in the last few months actually." I let the words drift out over the lawn. "I thought I was in love and that out turned to be crap. I thought I had the team, and that blew up in my face."

"Oh man, love?"

"I don't want to talk about it."

"We never do, unless it's good."

"I don't know, I guess I thought senior year would be so different and all it's been is a disappointment."

"You're on the negative coaster, little man, you got to find the positive."

I think of Charlie sitting with me in the car tonight. I think of Tommy not asking me to leave him alone today.

"I did make new friends."

"Alright, there's a start. If you dance with the devil long enough, you'll only get burnt. And trust me, the devil is a great dancer. She's sexy as hell and she lets you wallow in your pity, but then you miss out on all the other things happening around you. You don't notice. You just keep dancing and before you know it, all the wallowing defines you. It owns you."

"Larry, what the hell are you talking about?" I look at him and see that he's slouched over the side of his chair. I look to the ground and count ten beer cans. Another bad night for him.

"Just be proud of yourself. That's all I'm saying. It's the hardest thing to do when things aren't breaking your way," he says, slurring his words.

"Alright, Larry, I'm proud of me. Now let's get you to bed." I help him to his feet and walk him to his room.

I spend most of Sunday in bed.

I have the worst case of the Monday blues. I should have stayed home and laid under my comforter the entire day. Usually, everyone meets up around my locker, but this morning no one is here. I haven't received a single text from anyone.

I guess I expected everyone to be looking at me with the same anger Tim has, but mostly people say, "good game" and "sorry you guys lost." It's unexpected and kind of nice. Even the teachers are saying nice things.

By the time I reach math, I'm starting to dread lunch. I can't sit at my normal spot. I guess I could skip going to the cafeteria and try to eat in the hallway instead. When Charlie comes into class, I think about asking her if I could crash her lunch table since we're heading there next. I can't bring myself to say the words out loud to her. It's too pathetic.

Mr. Todd passes back our tests we took on Thursday. He paces the aisle, handing each one personally to the students. He stops at my desk and places his hand on my shoulder.

"You're really doing well," he says and lays my test on my desk. A+.

I stare at the red ink in amazement. I thought I bombed this test and here in front of me is an A+.

"Charlie," I whisper. "What did you get?"

"A-," she says, holding the paper up. "Tom is going to be so proud of us."

"We have to find him."

"At lunch. Why don't you sit with me today?" she asks.

"Okay, I will."

After I buy my lunch, I walk toward the area Charlie told me to find her. Out of the corner of my eye, I see Tim and company laughing at the table I'm supposed to be at. I swallow my anger and keep moving further away from them. Don't dance with the devil or whatever bullshit Larry was saying Saturday night.

"Holy crap!" Charlie says when I sit. "How many chocolate milks can you drink?"

"Milk make strong bone," I say in my best Russian accent.

"But four milks make boy into cow," she mimics me.

"Moooo."

I situate my tray with all my milks lined up above my plate. It's funny how no one even questions my presence at their table. Paige smiles at me as she grabs Charlie's bag of chips off her tray and offers me some. If any of them showed up at my old table, they probably would leave immediately because no one would have made them feel welcomed. It makes me sick to know that is the truth, and I followed along by never thinking there was another option. I wonder what else or who else I missed out on all these years by keeping my head tucked down.

The group is talking about going into the city this weekend for some pop-up art show. I eat and listen to them, thinking about how much different they sound from what I'm used to.

"Do you want to go, Duke? It would be your first bus ride." Charlie is looking intently at me.

"Will you hold my hand on the bus and make sure I get back home to my mom and dad?"

"No, I won't. I'm going to make sure we lose you and you're left in the city all alone."

"That's not very nice of you, but I'm in," I say, taking the brownie she is about to eat out of her hand.

"Hey," she cries in protest. "Fine. I'll make sure you get home safe and sound. Now give me my brownie back."

"Deal." I break a small piece off, popping it into my mouth before handing it back.

"That's an edible, dummy," she says. "Enjoy the high."

"What?" I look around to see if any of the cafeteria aids are watching us.

"Just messing with you," she says, laughing as if it were the funniest thing ever.

"You're so funny, Charlie," I say, smiling because it feels like I've always sat here with these people.

They continue talking as I scan the cafeteria, looking for Tommy. I can't wait to show him my A+. It dawns on me that I don't even know if he has lunch this period.

When the bell rings, we stand and clear our table.

"See you at tutoring," Charlie says.

"See you there."

The rest of the day drags on. Each minute feels like twenty-four hours have passed. When the final bell rings, I rush out of class.

I find Charlie sitting at our usual table but she's alone. Tommy is never late, but then again, I did sort of run here with my test in my hand.

"Where's Tommy?" I ask, taking a seat next to Charlie.

"I don't know. I haven't seen him all day. I didn't think he missed school ever, and of all days when his students get As on their test."

"I was thinking of taking him out to dinner later to celebrate." I look around, hoping to find him.

"You have to wait for me. I have to work today, but we can go tomorrow."

"Oh shit, I forgot I have to clean out my football locker. Tomorrow it is."

"Want to play hangman while we wait?" she asks, opening her notebook.

"Or maybe we can play Tic Tac Toe?" I say, laughing at her.

"You could never beat me in Tic Tac Toe."

"Please," I say, drawing the board.

We play for a good while, long enough to get mad that she's crushing me. We finally leave when tutoring would have ended.

I walk the empty hallways to the locker room. How many times have I done this walk? Too many to count. But none have ever felt this lonely, this final.

Mostly everyone's locker has been gutted and the locker door left open for Coach to do locker checks. I open mine and feel a wave of sadness. Tim should be next to me. His locker is bare. I wonder when he cleaned it out and if he was sad that I wasn't there. There isn't much left in my locker. Just the play book, extra mouth guards, and some clothes. I quickly clean it out and leave.

"Duke, wait up," I hear Smookler say.

"I didn't know you were still here."

"I've been waiting for you."

"Why?"

"Because," he says and pauses. "I wanted to."

We walk down the hallway to the back doors. "You need a lift home?"

"Actually, I do."

When he pulls up to my house, he puts the car in park.

"I don't know why Tim's being such a dick. It's not like he won't get into college because we lost the playoff game."

"He has his reasons," I say, not entirely sure of what I mean.

"I don't get it. But we're cool?" He looks over at me.

"We're cool."

"The party sucked without you."

"I'm sure it was fun," I say, not hiding my bitterness.

"Maybe it was, but it wasn't the same."

I open the door and say goodbye, not wanting to talk anymore about the things I missed out on.

After dinner, I finish my homework in my bedroom. It feels so weird not having practice take up so much time in my day. I throw on my television and play *Madden* to stop myself from thinking. I'm startled when my phone goes off because it's been so quiet lately.

"Miss me already?" I say, picking up Charlie's call.

"Tom's in the hospital. It's bad. That girl, Roxy, came to the coffee house asking everyone if they knew you. When I said I did, she told me to tell you that you should go see him."

"What?"

"Duke, focus, can you come pick me up?"

"Yes. I'll be there in a few minutes."

THE SECONDARY WRECK: IN BETWEEN

TOMMY: AGE 17

In the darkness, I hear her voice. She is singing, I think. She used to sing all the time when I was little, so young, I barely remember, but hearing her voice now is like standing in the kitchen on Dale Ave watching her work the grill cheeses on the stovetop and singing along with the radio.

I call to her, but she doesn't answer so I follow her voice.

"There you are, Tommy, I got so scared."

Somehow, we are standing in the living room of the last apartment we lived in. Her makeup has smeared down from her eyes as if she was crying black tears that left little trails of sadness along the way.

"I was calling your name, why didn't you come?" She's in the same clothes she walked out of the house two nights ago in. "Didn't you hear me?"

I say nothing.

She is wobbling like the floor is the ocean and she is a little tugboat lost in a big wave. First, she looks through me, and then she looks right at me.

"I'm sorry I had to leave you alone. I had to take care of a few things. You understand, right?"

My voice is cemented deep in my chest, unwilling or unable to break free. I desperately want to hug her, but I can't figure out how to move.

"Are you not talking to me, Tommy?" Her question bounces off me, making her lose interest in me.

I watch as she walks to the sofa and flops down.

She turns the fan on and adjusts it so it's hitting her directly on the face. She dumps the contents of her purse onto the coffee table and digs around to find her cigarettes and lighter. Only after a few drags does she remember that I'm still standing in the room. She almost looks surprised to see me.

"It's so hot in here. You should have turned this fan on. Remember the summer rule, fans always on. And what's that smell?" She looks at me. "It smells like piss. Tommy, did you pee yourself?"

I nod.

"And you didn't change? Did you sit on the furniture?" Her voice grows angry and matches her scary makeup face.

I'm shaking.

"Go clean yourself up, now," she demands, jamming her cigarette out into the ashtray. "I can't even be near you like that."

"It was an accident," I say, so quietly I didn't think she heard me.

"Accidents don't happen at your age."

The living room grows dark and I'm left alone again, floating in a sea of murky water. I don't want to be alone. I call out and there is no answer.

DUKE

I stare at the paused players on the television screen. I know I need to get up and go, but since I hung up with Charlie, it feels like someone poured wet concrete all over my body and it's already drying.

Her voice digs into my ears. Tom's in the hospital. It's bad. But it can't be bad. I wish I knew Roxy better to know whether or not she exaggerates, but something about her makes me think she doesn't and she means what she says. It's bad.

I grab the pair of pants I left on the floor and change out of my sweats.

Down the hallway, I find my parents in the living room.

"I need to borrow the car."

"Why?" Mom asks, muting the television.

"Tommy is in the hospital and Charlie wants me to pick her up so we can go see him."

"Is everything okay?" Dad asks.

"I think so," I lie. I can't tell him that some strange girl thinks it's bad and I really need to get there fast. That will only make Mom question my driving skills, and then one of them will have to escort us there.

"My keys are on the table," he answers.

"Thank you," I say, turning to leave.

"Tell him we hope he gets better fast," Mom says, her voice floating down the hallway after me.

In the car, I am speeding to the coffee house. I know I need to drive more carefully so I tap the brakes and feel the car slow down, which makes me aware that I am wasting time so I speed up again. I do this all the way to Charlie. Fast, then slow. Just like my brain. The thoughts of something really bad happening to Tommy speed up like a bullet released from its chamber. But then I think that can't be true and I picture him at the lunch table annoyed I'm late and my brain slows down.

Charlie is waiting on the sidewalk. I pull over and let her in.

"You got here fast," she says, sliding into the passenger seat. "This is his room number." She pulls out a crumpled napkin from her coat pocket.

I pull back on the road and steady my foot on the gas pedal.

"What happened?" I ask.

"I don't know. It was really busy at work and that girl Roxy didn't go into any details. She just said I needed to tell you and then she left. I wanted to follow her, but I had some douche bag complaining that his vanilla latte wasn't latte enough—whatever that means. Anyway, she was gone and I didn't see where she went."

"But she said it was bad?"

"Yeah." Her voice is so soft I almost don't hear it.

"It's probably nothing," I say more to assure me than to assure her.

"We won't know if you keep driving like an old lady."

I glance over at her and realize that it wasn't a joke. I can see her face, twisted up like she ate something sour, and her hands are balled into little fists. I step on the gas.

THE SECONDARY WRECK: IN BETWEEN

TOMMY: AGE 17

Nan is by the back door, waiting with her winter coat on. Outside, the sky looks grey dotted with bare, brown branches that seem to shiver against a cold breeze. The earth is still frozen, though the snow from the last storm has melted away. It is pruning day.

"Why can't you wait for warm weather?" I ask her. It is the first winter I've lived here.

"Are you changing your mind about helping me?" She looks at me, a small look, but I can see a little disappointment.

"I'm coming." I grab my coat from off the hook and follow her outside. In the garage, Pop is tinkering around on one of his work tables. He looks up as we enter through the open garage door. Nan grabs her gardening bucket that is tucked on her gardening shelf. "Have fun," he yells as we walk out.

We sit on the ground around her favorite rose bushes. She points out the dead that we need to trim off.

"You want to keep about three or four strong stems for each bush." She takes hold of the shears and snips away. "The dead makes the plant sick and if you don't cut it out, you won't get a beautiful rose bush. And you do it at the end of winter before it can bloom, to answer your question from before."

I work away as the cold settles into my bones. I take off my gloves, fearing that the bulkiness would make me sloppy while trying to cut away at the tiny branches, but I'm left with little cuts from the thorns.

I can't imagine why anyone would love a plant so much that makes you bleed and makes you tend to it in the bitterness of winter.

"Roses have many meanings, did you know that?" She looks at me and sighs when she sees my hands. "Put your gloves back on, Tommy."

"It's too late. I'm already bleeding."

"It's never too late to stop getting cuts. You'll get the hang of this. We have to do it every winter."

"Every winter?" I look at her and see that she is laughing at me.

"The only way this can grow bigger and stronger is if you take the time to nurture and love it. Once you see these roses in the spring, you'll understand the sacrifice is worth the beauty."

"I guess." I focus back on my work.

"Well, I'll appreciate it for the both of us."

We work and work and work. I am frozen to the core. I want nothing more than to feel the warm sun against my skin. It's getting darker. "Nan," I say, but she isn't there anymore.

DUKE

We arrive at the hospital and navigate our way to the help desk. They confirm the floor and room number. Charlie reeks like coffee. It's all I can think about as I follow her down the crisp white hallways. This place is a maze.

When we get to his room, his grandparents are sitting in chairs next to his bed. They look so tired as they watch him. They look nothing like the two people I met in the garage a few days ago. The sound of the machine's beeping is too loud for me. The sight of Tommy with tubes shoved down his throat is choking me inside out.

When his grandparents see us standing in the doorway, their faces light up. They give us giant hugs and hold on extra tight.

"What happened?" I ask as we stand in a semi-circle away from Tommy. It feels like we are keeping a secret from him.

"He must have been leaning against the rotting railing and it gave way," Pop answers. "He broke his fall with the back of his head. He's in a coma now and they aren't sure if he'll come out of it." He takes a long breath. "Only time will tell."

"You must be Charlie," Tommy's grandma says.

"I am," Charlie answers.

I lose focus on what they are talking about and look at Tommy. *I should have asked you more questions, should have cared more to get to know you, instead of selfishly talking about me the whole time.*

I just want to take it all back. I want a redo.

I'm sorry. I'm sorry. I'm sorry.

"Why don't you guys sit with him for a little bit? The doctors say it's good to talk to him," Pop says. "We'll grab a cup of coffee and be right back."

We watch them leave and pull the chairs up close to his bed.

"Now what?" I ask.

"We talk to him."

I look at him lying there and wonder if he can even hear us. I can talk to Larry for hours when I know he's not really listening to me, but this seems different. Maybe it's because Charlie is here, or maybe it's because it seems like whatever I say to him needs to be important. And I have nothing important to say.

Charlie tells him about our As, as if any of that matters now. She looks at me as if I am going to talk and shrugs when she realizes that I'm not. She tells him the story about us crashing the party and how she's going to take me to the city and maybe he can come on the next trip when he's better. She's really good at filling the silence.

I stare at the machine that keeps watch of him, terrified that I'll see his heart rate flat line.

THE SECONDARY WRECK: IN BETWEEN

TOMMY: AGE 17

I follow the sunshine. It's so bright my eyes can barely focus, but when they do, I see the willow tree, and Roxy lying under it. I walk over to her and lie next to her.

"Tommy, do you think that the mice go to heaven?"

I look at her; she has little tears trickling from her eyes.

"I hope so," she says. "I hope they get up there and are free to run around with no one trying to trap them on glue boards, or worse the ones that snap down and break their necks. I hope there is a giant block of cheese and whatever else mice like."

I look up into the branches of the tree and think of how big that cheese block would be and wonder if mice can smile.

"It's just not fair that they die when they have a whole life to live. You know what I mean, Tommy? Imagine if you were just walking down the street one day and then you were suddenly stuck to a glue board?"

The thought terrorizes me.

"If I were stuck on a glue board, Tommy, I would want you to sit near me. You can't touch me because then you'll get stuck, but promise you won't leave me alone."

"I would never leave you," I say. We lie under the tree for hours.

DUKE

"Oh, sorry am I interrupting?" Roxy says, coming through the door. She looks different from the last time I saw her. Instead of wearing all black, she's in a pair of jeans and a sweatshirt. She's really pretty, something I didn't notice the last time I saw her.

"Not at all," Charlie says.

"You're the girl from the coffee house," Roxy says, her voice sounding a little harsh, like Charlie is some kind of threat. She studies Charlie, and I feel the need to say something but don't.

"I'm friends with Tom too."

"I didn't know that," Roxy answers, giving a weak smile as she walks toward us.

For a moment we lock eyes and I know that she's not mad like the first time I met her.

She sits on the end of the bed and squeezes his hands.

"This is crazy," I say.

"It is," Roxy says.

"Can I ask you something?" I say, looking at Roxy. "Why was he at your place?"

"He showed up on his own," she answers.

A little sting of rejection pulses through my heart. Or maybe relief. It's not my fault that he is like this. Roxy didn't listen to me and realize she was being an idiot for turning Tommy away. She didn't call him and invite him over. I'm not to blame.

But that's not it either. I sit back in my chair, feeling desperate for fresh air. Maybe I did want Roxy to call Tommy. Not for the credit. No. I wanted to give Tommy something important: his friend back.

"He came to give some stuff he was holding on to for me. It was nice." Roxy looks me over, then settles her gaze back on Tommy.

I think of Tim and wonder what it will be like to not have him as a friend anymore. Maybe I never had him as a friend in the first place. Roxy said that her and Tommy's friendship was based on proximity and that pissed me off because it couldn't be true that friendship could only be as thick as location or sports.

The room settles back into silence, but my mind is busier than ever, replaying all the shit that has happened in the last few weeks.

"I can't believe how stupid life is," I say, looking at Tommy. "All we do is worry about the dumbest stuff ever. And in the end, none of it matters."

"Some of it matters," Charlie says. "This matters. You matter. Tommy matters."

"Of course, Tommy matters. I just mean all the other crap."

"The trivial crap," Roxy chimes in.

"Right," I say. "How many nights did I waste hoping Kristy would text me? Too many. How many times did I let my sister down? Countless. How many minutes did I walk around thinking I was the shit? Immeasurable."

"When you put it like that, I guess you're right," Charlie says. "Maybe you suffer from an inflated ego."

"Shut up, Charlie," I say, feeling good to smile even if for a minute.

We sit and watch Tommy like lifeguards watching the surf.

"He is a good friend," Roxy finally says, mostly to herself.

"I can't remember the last words I said to him," I say, trying hard to remember.

"He's not dying, Duke," Charlie yells. "He can't."

I look at her and see she's crying. I reach out and hold her hand. Somewhere along the line, she and Tommy became my favorite people. I grab Tommy's hand.

"We're supposed to talk to him. So, let's talk," I say. "The first time I met you, Tommy, I didn't like you."

"How is that helping?" Charlie asks.

"I meant that I didn't want to be tutored at all. But then it turned out to be something that I kind of looked forward to. You made it way more fun than I thought it could be."

"You are the worst at using your words," Charlie interrupted. "Tom, the best thing that happened to me this year was failing math and ending up with you and Duke. I need you to wake up so we can continue what we started."

"That's almost exactly what I said." I look at Charlie for confirmation.

"Not even close," she says, her face twisted in disgust. "Your turn, Roxy."

"I don't think so," Roxy answers, shaking her head. "That's between me and Tommy."

"Fair enough," I say. Her words sound like a warning shot, and I'm not about to argue with her. "We're all right here, Tommy," I say. "And we'll be here waiting for you. Whatever it is that you're going through, you're not going through it alone. You hear me, Tommy?"

THE SECONDARY WRECK: ENDINGS

TOMMY: AGE 17

I hear you, Duke.

ACKNOWLEDGMENTS

A huge thank you to Tina P Schwartz of the Purcell Agency for believing in me and supporting me over the years. It's amazing how one simple phone call can change your life. I'm so thankful I get to take this journey with you.

Thank you to Reagan Rothe Creator of Black Rose Writing for taking me into your family of amazing and talented authors.

They say that writing a novel is a lonely task which in many ways is true. But what I've learned on my journey is that you are never alone. Thank you, Helen W. Mallon, for running the best writing critique group. You are an incredible writer, teacher, and mentor.

And of course, I have to thank my amazing friend Deidra Norris for always, and I mean always, reading every word to every manuscript I have ever tried writing! You have been extremely kind with your time and cheered me on even when I felt like giving up. A simple thank you isn't enough for all the support you have given to me. I am forever grateful for our friendship. To Erin Scharff, my co-conspirator in mischief since high school and a constant sounding boarding for far too many years than I would like to acknowledge! Thank you for going to New York City for years, so I could attend the SCBWI conference in the dead of winter. You and Deidra made those unbearably cold nights traversing through Manhattan more fun than any of us could have ever imagined. Two deep on the wall for life. Denise Wolf, you have been my reading and world examining buddy since the first day I met you. Just one conversation with you could spark an entire novel. I love that we have never given up our teenage angst- us against the world. Luckily, we found each other so when the world occasionally wins, we can pick each other up. To Jim Wood, let it be known that I am the lucky one to have met you. The support and love you give to me is immeasurable.

Mom and Dad, you never once gave up on me when I was diagnosed with Dyslexia. You made me believe in me. You were full of love and praise and instilled toughness and grit in me that has carried me through life. I was the underdog and you showed me how to fight. You taught me how to get back up when I failed and I failed more often than I ever succeeded, but you made sure to remind me that living meant that failure was part of the deal. This particular lesson has proven to be the one thing that kept me writing when the rejections came. To my sister Jen, her husband Eric, and children, Erin, Jake, Ella, and Zack -you guys are simply the best. Jen, thank you for being the best sister- from all of our juvenal fights to the big wonderful moments in life you have been a rock. To my brother John- oh the trouble we got into! I am so lucky to have grown up with a big brother who is also my best friend. You have always had my back, which meant I could take big risks in my life and know I had someone in my corner. Your advice and guidance since the day I was born has shaped me into who I am today. I love you all.

And to you, dear reader, whatever you dream to become may the journey be the adventure.

Never be discouraged when the tides pull you in different directions- be open, be in awe, be inspired.

\

ABoUT THE AUTHoR

Lynn Langan lives in Bucks County, Pennsylvania. She graduated from Kutztown University with a degree in Professional Writing.

NOTE FROM THE AUTHOR

Word-of-mouth is crucial for any author to succeed. If you enjoyed *Duke & The Lonely Boy*, please leave a review online—anywhere you are able. Even if it's just a sentence or two. It would make all the difference and would be very much appreciated.

Thanks!
Lynn Langan

Thank you so much for checking out one of our **Young Adult Fiction** novels.
If you enjoy our book, please check out our recommended title for your next great read!

What the Valley Knows by Heather Christie

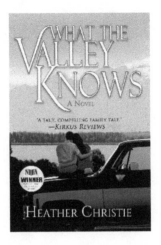

"A taut, compelling family tale." –
KIRKUS REVIEWS